The Sailor from Casablanca

Charline Malaval was born in Limoges in 1984, and grew up in Corrèze, south-western France. Having worked in Brazil, Mauritius, Bulgaria and Vanuatu, she now teaches at the French Lycée in Riga. *The Sailor from Casablanca* is her first novel.

The Sailor from Casablanca

CHARLINE MALAVAL

Translated from the French
by Natasha Lehrer

HODDER

First published in the French language as *Le Marin de Casablanca*
by Librairie Générale Française in 2019

First published in Great Britain in 2020 by Hodder & Stoughton
An Hachette UK company

1

A CIP catalogue record for this title is available from the British Library

Paperback ISBN 9781529351651
eBook ISBN 9781529351675

Typeset in Plantin Light by
Palimpsest Book Production Ltd, Falkirk, Stirlingshire

Printed and bound in Great Britain by Clays Ltd, Elcograf S.p.A.

Hodder & Stoughton policy is to use papers that are natural, renewable
and recyclable products and made from wood grown in sustainable forests.
The logging and manufacturing processes are expected to conform
to the environmental regulations of the country of origin.

Hodder & Stoughton Ltd
Carmelite House
50 Victoria Embankment
London EC4Y 0DZ

www.hodder.co.uk

To Eugénie

The past is never dead. It's not even past.

William Faulkner

I

They Call Me the Comeback Kid

Felix, 1940

I'm not saying I was going to do a runner or anything, but my heart was in my boots and I felt like I was standing on the edge of a cliff . . . Announcing someone's death was no one's idea of fun. But dying like that, so young, in such circumstances . . . that was just rotten luck.

I reckoned Guillaume would've known what to say. He'd have managed to adopt just the right expression, anyway, and he'd have come out with some line from a film that hit just the right note, like he always did, always so sure of himself. He'd have had them eating out of his hand, and made them cry at just the right amount.

Still, we couldn't exactly ask the poor bastard to organize his own farewell party, and then write his own eulogy to boot!

It was the hardest bloody thing I'd ever had to do in my life. Joining the navy, saying goodbye to my old dad and his cows, kissing my weeping mother in the early morning and heading off out of Meaux . . . that was nothing compared to this.

I'd had the whole journey back from Morocco to prepare myself, waiting around in the railway station, getting from Toulon to Paris and then the bus to Amiens, but my thoughts were still all over the place, wondering what was going to happen when the words blundered out of my mouth.

I had no idea how to tell them, Guillaume's parents. I knew it was best to keep it simple, that *He's dead. I'm sorry*, was all I really needed to say, because that was the brutal truth, there was nothing more to add. But damn it, I couldn't do it.

Pulling myself together, I told myself, "Felix, you're going to go to their house, and you're going to tell them. If they offer you a coffee, you're going to sip it ever so politely. If they ask you questions, don't say anything . . . Just fudge it, as the saying goes – end of story. Then you can get back to enjoying your leave and sinking a few in honour of your old mate."

I walked through the garden gate and spotted his mother, Hélène, out of the corner of my eye. She saw me from where she was standing on the front steps, with my uniform and my cap with its red pompom under my arm, because I knew I should uncover my head out of respect. It was my mate Eugène who told me I should go in this way. "If you turn up in your uniform you won't even have to say it, '*Your son is dead.*' A sentence like that can fell you for days, going round and round your head." He wasn't wrong. For parents, the death of a son is quite sad enough; there's no need to make it worse by adding words that will just linger long after they've been spoken. And oh God, of course he was right, there was no need to say anything in the end. She wasn't expecting me, so when I turned up it was pretty obvious I wasn't bringing good news; she understood immediately.

Before I'd even got close to the front steps, her knees buckled and she collapsed. Luckily at the last minute she grabbed at the front door, or she'd have smashed her head on the stone. She stared at me, eyes and mouth wide open, then she uttered an awful cry. I can't imagine the horrors that were going through her head, but they must have been at least as bad as my worst nightmares.

Lying there on the ground, Hélène began to howl like a wounded animal. In the whole of my short life I'd never imagined I'd be responsible for causing so much pain.

I wasn't exactly feeling wonderful myself, and now the one thing I wanted was to run away as fast as I could . . . but I forced myself to have the courage to stand there and face the effect that I would have on the whole family.

His father Lucien must have heard the screaming as he suddenly appeared and tried to help her up. She pulled her arm away and threw him a furious look. She didn't want him to touch her; bad luck is contagious. It looked like she wanted to be alone on the front steps with her grief.

The poor bastard just stood there, holding out his hand, no idea what to do . . . It was probably easier for him to stare at her than to accept it was all over. After a moment, long enough to get over the initial bombshell, Hélène seemed to pull herself together, and shock and pain gave way to complete calm. The best way I can find to describe it is that it was like she had found relief from some terrible torment. As if this had put an end to all their questions and doubts. Even when it comes to the worst possible thing, it's always better to know than not to know.

I decided that if I was going to go up and introduce myself, it was now or never. But I wanted to hold off for a minute rather than say something straight off, so I held out the letter I'd been given to hand over to them, typed by Captain Hourcade himself.

Obviously I hadn't read it, but I think it said everything that needed to be said. In other words, not quite the whole truth. Broadly speaking, yes; but there are things that civilians aren't supposed to know, and I'd been well briefed in that regard. "Felix, you must give them the official version. And the official version is that we don't know anything. The only thing we know is, it's wartime and their boy gave his life for France. And that's all they need to know, too." As he read the letter, Lucien stood there, tall and dignified. It's quite something to find yourself in front of an impressive man like that, a man who'd endured the Nivelle Offensive in 1917 and hadn't been sent home feet first. It would've been incredible in any circumstances. Guillaume had told me all about his father's feats in the Great War: he'd skewered some Germans, when it was a question of him or them. But apparently he never talked about the massacre. He just used to say that you had to draw on all the strength you had if you wanted to come back in one piece – there was nothing to do but to focus on that one thing. Guillaume always told us his father was born under a lucky star. He came back from the trenches without a scratch, and that must mean it was in Guillaume's blood as well. "I'll be the last man standing, you'll see. I'm like my dad – they call me the Comeback Kid." He should've kept his trap shut, poor bastard.

But even though he'd thought he was hard as nails, and bound to survive, that doesn't mean it should have happened the way it did. The whole thing made you want to smash your head against a wall, it was so bloody pointless.

I stood watching them, and in spite of everything, it was quite something how his parents maintained their dignity. It suddenly hit me what a big deal it was to have been Guillaume's friend, how much I'd taken him for granted . . . I might have been able to make a difference if I'd met them earlier.

It made me so sad to think of the void Guillaume had left behind him. With some people it wouldn't really have been a big deal. Me, for example. You might've felt some affection for me, I'm not saying you wouldn't, but with him it was so much more. It really felt like he was going places . . . he wasn't just hanging around patiently till it was his turn to peg it. He was on his way somewhere, somewhere better, somewhere great! You just knew it. But all the same, you never felt like he was looking down on you.

But damn it . . . that day it was either him or me. And things weren't great for me now. It was all about to kick off again. My leave would be over in three weeks and I was going to have to go back, without my friend Guillaume . . . Because that's how it was; we were up to our necks in it now. We could no longer fool ourselves into thinking that we were going to escape war, that we were going to "stick it to the Krauts".

I met Guillaume back in 1936, on basic training in Toulon. We were both from the north and we hit it off right away. He was awfully young. Much younger than the rest of us, but he'd got some kind of dispensation . . . Which made him sound so serious, what with the rest of us wishing we could've got a dispensation to get out of the navy. But we didn't tease him for long. There was nothing accidental about him being there. He was a really determined lad.

He talked about going off to see the world. He was bored as hell in Toulon, the whole way through basic training. He said he knew enough for them to let him jump in the big blue – that's what we called the Mediterranean.

At first all he would talk about was the size of the world, and he'd read so many books that he talked like one. But he was a real character too, and he manned the guns like nobody else. And even when the ship pitched and rolled, he wasn't the kind of bloke to throw up over the side.

I can still picture him, surrounded by all his books, lying on his bunk, one arm folded behind his head. That was when we used to really talk. He was so self-possessed. He knew all these adventure stories and travel tales: "The world is so vast, Felix, too vast to be content with just gawping at the horizon. You have to embrace it, drink it all up, to the very last drop." That was the way he always talked.

He was handsome, well brought up, good-natured. Sometimes I used to think I didn't belong in the same cabin. He loved reading, but what he loved more than anything was the flicks.

If you didn't understand Guillaume's passion for the cinema, you didn't really understand who he was. It was all he ever thought about. It was very simple – as soon as we got to shore, in Toulon, Casablanca, Bizerte, Algiers, the first thing he'd do was find his way to the nearest cinema. He'd watch anything. French films, American, Italian . . . he'd go and see them all. But his favourite was anything that starred Jean Gabin.

Ah, my old friend! He wouldn't have missed the latest Gabin for anything. He could recite whole scenes from his films by heart; it was amazing to watch.

With his accent from the north, it sounded even better. Almost as good as the straight-talking Parisian whippersnapper scrambling over the rooftops. He had a mouth on him, that's for sure. I think he really identified with Gabin, especially when he read that Gabin had been drafted by the navy in Cherbourg.

Guillaume saw this as a sign. He used to say he was going to follow Gabin's lead – he was going to get out of the navy and try his luck in the pictures.

That's what he wanted to do when he got out of prison – that's what he'd begun calling the navy. "I'm going to give it a go." Anytime some newsperson showed up, he'd make sure he was caught on film, so there might be a glimpse of him in the newsreel before the feature. "They're going to see me in a hundred cinemas, Felix. That's how it's done. How else do you think people get spotted?"

When he thought he looked good in a photograph, he'd send it to the newspapers. One time, *Le Frou-Frou* printed one. He was pretty chuffed. He was bound to end up doing something big. He had it all: the looks, the confidence, the charisma . . . He was going to blow them away, that young lad from the Somme region. And he was nobody's fool, either.

I wasn't like that. I didn't have big dreams – I didn't have time for them. In Meaux, when I was young, I had to look after the animals for my parents and grandparents. I enlisted so I could send a bit of money home and get some experience of the world, but I can't say I'm any happier to be in the navy than slogging my guts out for some employer in town. At least there I learned a trade, electrician. Now it was the sea that was giving me a thrashing. There's always something to keep you from getting too big for your boots.

When I finally make it home – *if* I make it home – I'll go back to it. And Christ, that suits me just fine.

Me and the other lads had a lot of respect for Guillaume, for the way he believed in himself so stubbornly. The confidence he had. Because when you want something that much, it doesn't half put some grand ideas into your head.

He couldn't take his eyes off the horizon, though you can't help feeling melancholy after you've stared at it for a while. It gets rid of all those grand ideas, for a start. And then, without you even noticing it creeping up, you're hit by such a wave of melancholy that you have no choice but to bawl your eyes out.

Whenever I said that to him, it made him smile. He'd tell me he liked feeling a bit melancholy, and that it was fate that made him melancholy more than staring at the horizon ever would . . . In any case it suited him, because in the films he loved most there was always some unlucky bastard whose life was a bit of a mess. Apart from that, I didn't really get the appeal.

The first time we docked in Casablanca after we were done with our basic training, he was obsessed by one thing: going to the Vox to see a film. He wasn't the only lad to be obsessed by one thing, but the rest of us had something a bit different in mind. We wanted to go to Bousbir, the red-light district. We all wanted to have a go with the famous "snake charmers".

It was a long time since any of us had so much as touched a woman, and we'd heard there was a plentiful supply of them there. People talked about them as far away as Marseille. There's a similar neighbourhood there as well, but to say it's not exactly chic would be an understatement. Marseille is dark, dangerous, sleazy . . . women yelling and brawling like fishwives, the sound of drunks and cheap music . . . It's squalid, full of whores and dirty money. Admittedly I'm no looker, but even I know you have to get away quick from these places, or you're bound to catch something.

That particular evening I was planning on heading out to Bousbir, but Guillaume had been bending my ear so much, going on about this cinema, that I began to think that if I didn't go it would be like not having seen the *Titanic* before it sank, and kicking yourself afterwards. So I ended up going with him.

It was 1938 and they were showing a Gabin film. Even though we'd already seen it because it'd come out in France the year before, we were happy to see it again. It was *Pépé le Moko*, the story of a lowlife smuggler, who underneath it all is really a good guy. He's a "Moko" like us, a lad from Toulon; ex-navy; who found himself on the wrong side of the tracks . . . Now he's got the police on his tail, and he's gone to ground in a casbah in Algiers. He can't come out or he might get nicked. So, obviously, he falls in love with a sophisticated lady

and now he can only dream of one thing: getting out . . . And
it's his dreams of escape that do for him in the end, even more
than if he'd got a bullet in the head.

I remember that night like it was yesterday. Guillaume was
getting dressed up in his civvies and he said to me: "You can't
go out in uniform, Felix! We're having a night on the town.
And where we're going, they don't want to see that we're not
quite as peace-loving as everyone likes to pretend we are."

So we left the port in our Sunday best, and ambled up the
Boulevard de la Gare. By the time we got there I'd already
attracted my fair share of glances, and I felt pretty good. It was
all so fancy. Guillaume had been right to tell me not to go out
dressed like a cabin boy; there were so many beautiful people
on this gorgeous avenue, it brought tears to my eyes. There
was no need to feel homesick any more because we could have
been in Paris, what with all the little cafés and tall white buildings. Only the palm trees down the middle reminded us that
such a mild March was the preserve of warmer climes. I walked
as confidently as I could, because alongside Guillaume I felt
like a bit of a peasant. I was used to that, but even so I wanted
to try and rise to his level. "Will you look at that!" I said. "Over
there – now that cinema is a beauty. The Empire. Oh my
goodness, there's another one! See the one on the left, the
Rialto? That's a real stunner!" Guillaume was in heaven. But
he was still focused on one thing: seeing the biggest cinema in
Africa. The Vox. He'd read about it in a newspaper in Toulon,
that it seated two thousand people and had three balconies.

We looked up, to the right, the left . . . there was music,
dancing, laughter, champagne flowing like water, and we kept
on walking towards the Place de France. There it was, the Vox,
and it really was an amazing sight. It was absolutely huge. Even
in France, I'd never seen a cinema so big. Not that I'd been to
that many, but still. It was mammoth, that building.

I have to say, I didn't regret not going to Bousbir, especially
once I was comfortably settled into my seat with a freshly lit
cigarette, enjoying the cool evening breeze. The place was half

open to the sky, with a roof that opened up to make you feel as if you were outside. I'd never seen anything like it before. It's moments like that which remind me what a lucky bastard I am, really, to have experienced such things. I was thinking how we'd be able to tell our mates back in France how we'd gone to the flicks, sat in big, plush seats, comfortable as kings. I could already see myself bragging about it. Guillaume was lost in the film, imagining he was in Pépé's shoes, repeating Gabin's lines under his breath.

He didn't say anything when we went for a drink afterwards at the Café de l'Empire on the Boulevard de la Gare. I knew Guillaume; he was replaying the film over and over in his head. It was about that time that he first became preoccupied by the idea of being trapped in a dead-end situation.

Out of the blue I saw this look of despair in his eyes; he was muttering one of Pépé's lines from the film, like he'd figured something out, some great revelation:

"'You're afraid for your life?' 'What d'you think? It's the only one I have.'"

Loubna, 2005

I grew up without a father, on Alger Street in Casablanca, not far from the United Nations Square and the central market on Hassan II Boulevard. It was a neighbourhood on the outskirts of the city, where the streets were lined with buildings that had been a dazzling white once upon a time.

As kids in the eighties and nineties, we'd spent our childhood hanging out at the port, or playing hide-and-seek among the mountains of spices and fruit piled up on stalls in the market. When we got older we'd walk up Almohades Boulevard to the Hassan II mosque to watch the rabble-rousing kids hanging out together on the ramparts below. Poised above the Atlantic Ocean, they'd dare each other to see who could dive into the waves without ending up in a belly-flop. I can't count the number of times we watched the fishermen ploughing through the waves in their trawlers. How many times we played truant, burning ourselves to a crisp on the white-hot sands of the beaches along the Corniche Boulevard and beyond the lighthouse.

Now we're adults and we all have our own histories in this city, Casablanca the crowded, Casablanca, devourer of destinies, Casablanca the beautiful.

Except I know barely anything of mine; that's why I can't bring myself to leave this place. It hasn't told me everything. All I have are the dreams I've woven into the spaces between lies and silence. There are so many gaps in my past that my present is filled with gusts of air carrying just the faintest trace of perfume. It's like the apartment building where I grew up: blank as a pristine sheet of paper waiting to be written on.

Everything I know about my father, my grandfather and my

grandmother I heard from my mother, who bequeathed me a few sweet memories tinged with sadness. At the age of twenty-five she found herself bringing me up on her own, the love affair that brought me into the world now no more than a speck of dust floating in a ray of Casablanca sunshine. It's as if my family were cursed. I barely knew my father, and he never knew his parents. I come from a family where the ties of blood and the past have vanished without trace.

History repeated itself with a tragic inevitability. In each generation, every new birth was like a rupture with the past, an ellipsis. No one survived to parent the next generation. No one was left to pass on what had been.

That's what it is to be a blank page.

My name is Loubna. I am the only child of my mother, a teacher, and my father, who died in 1975, the year I was born. He never heard me talk. He never saw me walk. Barely had he planted a kiss on my forehead than he was no longer of this world.

Obviously this meant that I never had a chance to ask him all the questions that are eating away at me now. My mother has kept a few photos, but even the mention of him remains a source of endless sadness.

Yet his story is inextricably linked to the history of Morocco. During the last few decades Casablanca has been the centre of continuous political upheaval. My father's involvement with the Moroccan Communist Party cost him his life. The arrest and conviction, on 31 July 1973, of eighty-four far-left activists spurred him on in his commitment. He took part in demonstrations and increasingly assumed a leadership role. He was shot by a soldier during a riot. In 1977, 178 Marxist–Leninists were sentenced in Casablanca after a series of group trials. If he hadn't been killed several months earlier, he would almost certainly have been among them.

He was thirty-four when he died. Almost the same age as I am today. My father's father was twenty when he died. I imagine it is always strange to reach the age where one is older than one's parents ever were. To grow older than them is against nature.

The scant details I managed to glean as I was growing up were enough for me to forge an image of my father that was pure romantic fantasy. His taste in films, his political commitment and his addiction to coffee allowed me to convince myself that he would have taught me to think for myself and to question the rules.

But what crystallized the ideas I had of him from when I was a little girl, through my teenage years, and even as a young woman, was the loveliest gift my mother ever gave me: the story of an evening when she found him singing "As Time Goes By" softly to me as he rocked me to sleep. The iconic tune from his favourite film, *Casablanca*, in the legendary scene where Ingrid Bergman asks Sam to "play it". Apparently my father could never get over the unsettling juxtaposition of Bergman's candour and the cool beauty of her smile. He told my mother that the screenplay had been in gestation at the same time as he had, and that as a consequence it could not help but turn out to be a masterpiece.

Ever since I was a little girl, I have been trying to summon that feeling again; I've listened to the song with intense concentration, as if the melody might be hiding other secrets. Throughout my life I've pictured myself snuggled in his arms in the little apartment on Alger Street that my mother has never left. How, or thanks to whom, my father acquired it I have no idea. Sometimes I imagine him humming, tickling me with his beard, and I hope that was the very first time I laughed. Or I'm swaddled in a big blanket and grizzling because he's started to sing, but flat, and I like to imagine him laughing, in a first moment of complicity. Or I fantasize that his lullaby made me fall into the deepest sleep of my entire life, because I felt so secure and loved and the tune he was humming was such a sweet accompaniment to my newborn dreams.

Even when I was a little girl I used to watch the old films that my father loved, by all his favourite directors: Charlie

Chaplin, Hitchcock, Godard, Eisenstein, Frank Capra, Mankiewicz, Antonioni, Murnau. He was interested in all the different movements: the golden age of Hollywood, the French, Italian and Czech New Waves, Iranian *motafavet*, the cinema of the Soviet Union . . . What I loved most about these films was the sense that there was a bond between us that death couldn't break. I felt it really strongly whenever I laughed watching Chaplin's *The Great Dictator*, or trembled at Hitchcock's *Psycho* or *Rear Window*, or was thrilled by the ending of *Sunset Boulevard*. On the other hand, when at the age of ten I struggled with the opaque, meditative aesthetic of the great cinematic monuments of Eisenstein, Tarkovsky and Bondarchuk, I decided there and then that because my father had been a communist, and that was the cause which led to his death, I would reject everything that emanated from the cold USSR.

Later, with impeccable logic, I decided to focus my life on the cinema and make a career in it. My father had left enough money for my mother and me to lead a pleasant, middle-class existence in Casablanca, though we were still a long way from the absurd affluence of those *nouveau riche* Moroccans who'd made their fortune in advertising, petrol and agriculture. I didn't go to school at the Lycée Lyautey with the children of wealthy French expatriates. I didn't live in a big villa with a swimming pool on the slopes of the Anfa Hills. I didn't have wads of cash to spend on dinner at Sky 28. But there was nothing I lacked, not money or education, and certainly not love from my mother, who had coped with being single for many years, and taught me to be a self-sufficient and independent woman.

I enjoyed my studies, and after graduating I found a job as cultural adviser for the Company of Pre-war Casablanca Cinemas, which means that officially I'm in charge of the programming for the Rialto, the Empire, the Ritz and the ABC, in other words almost all the cinemas built before the Second World War, in the port area, Hassan II Boulevard and the neighbourhood around the United Nations Square. I help Djamel Terrab, my boss, manage his assets. Officially I'm his right-hand woman, but in reality I'm responsible for everything: the budget, employing the cleaners, ushers and technicians, buying material, and implementing the inevitable works and renovations. Djamel is completely uninterested in the practical issues to do with the smooth running of his cinemas, even though this family heritage is his prized possession.

His parents were architecture and film enthusiasts, and they acquired the cinema group in the wake of Morocco's independence. I have to say he's the best boss I could imagine. Obviously I do the job of four or five people, but he leaves me alone and supports my programming ideas, in spite of the fact that they aren't exactly designed to bring in the punters: a week of Italian New Wave films, a Tarkovsky retrospective, a festival of 1930s *film noir* – as long as I offset these screenings for dedicated film buffs with showings of the American blockbusters that the kids are so fond of.

When I was about twelve years old, a ritual was established. Every Wednesday and Saturday in the late afternoon I would go and order a large glass of freshly squeezed orange juice at my mother's friend Osman's café, then take it with me to one of the old cinemas that now belong to Djamel. After the film was over, I'd return the glass. That was when I first met Anis, Osman's son, who became my best friend, and often joined me.

A few years later (after Anis's father had begun to give us plastic glasses), a persistent idea began to take root in my mind. The cinemas had been built during the colonial period, in the 1920s and 30s, and were beginning, inevitably, to fall into a state of disrepair. The film and the orange juice, however good they were, were no longer enough to distract me from the buildings' musty, stale smell. I wanted my own cinema, whose cachet would lie in its perfect blend of elegant Casablanca art deco with traditional Moroccan style.

Djamel and I put together several applications for funding to the Ministry of Culture, but to no avail. The coffers of the Company of Pre-war Casablanca Cinemas weren't big enough to give me the leg-up I needed, bearing in mind the extent of the renovation work that would be required.

My father's birth defies all logic, for although he knew his father's identity, he never knew who his mother was. He was born in the Ben M'sik military hospital in 1940, but no one knew why his mother had been admitted there. War had only recently broken out, and tears of grief mingled with the agony of labour. My father's father was nowhere to be found. By some miracle the pregnancy had continued to term, even though my grandmother had almost completely stopped eating. She gave birth in the early morning, after a long night and a difficult labour. Far too weak to fight, and inconsolable with grief, she died soon after from complications related to the birth.

Before she died, she gave my father the name Tarek, meaning "morning light". She had told Zanya that she meant to pay homage not to her baby's first breath, but to her very first assignation with her lover in the port of Casablanca. I don't know if this fact constituted my father's first disappointment. It was Zayna, the nurse who helped my grandmother through her labour, who took the baby home and brought him up with her husband as their own son.

On her deathbed, which was also the bed where she gave birth, my grandmother kept repeating my grandfather's name, the name of the man she had loved so deeply.

She handed my adopted grandmother a bundle of notes, a huge sum of money for the time. That is literally all I know. Not a word more. Zayna never managed to find out the young woman's identity. Afterwards, the war consumed her. She spent the years tending to wounded sailors of every nationality who filed through the Ben M'sik hospital.

My father must have grown up as I did, cherishing the untarnished image of a single, unique embrace in the arms of his mother, who even on the brink of death still refused to give her name, and a father who had died or disappeared, whose name was Guillaume.

My grandfather, my grandmother and my father all died before they could bequeath me their passions, their ideas, their beliefs, the things about which they were proud or ashamed, their fantasies of how they might have done things better or differently. I have no idea what they lived through, what aspect of their experience I may have to grapple with at some point. All they've left me is a taste for the past, and specifically for the films of a certain era. When I sit down to watch one, I feel like I'm bringing to life something that is constantly slipping from my grasp.

No doubt that's why I ended up taking refuge in the cinema: film takes suffering, and lives full of uncertainty, and turns them into an art form. There's nothing more moving on screen than these absences and definitive endings. I dream in eighty-four images a second, and the history of my family has always seemed as intriguing and melancholy as a beautiful black and white film projected onto the screen at the Rialto after the heavy red velvet curtains glide open, ending on a cliffhanger whenever the first hint of romance seems about to develop. There are no happy endings, just goodbyes and missed connections.

Hélène, 1940

We weren't naïve, we knew perfectly well that the situation was growing increasingly tense. I couldn't stop thinking about my son and how, quite suddenly, he had become a man. In 1936 he left home, all starry-eyed, and a few months later he was playing with the big boys, having completed his first mission to Spain. That was in the early part of the civil war; two years later he watched as Barcelona was bombed right before his eyes.

Ah, these idiotic Spanish, when are they going to stop being at each other's throats? Spain has become a country filled with tragedy and horror. I'm sure it's an entirely unoriginal sentiment, and don't breathe a word to Father, but how I hate war . . .

If we'd known that it was just the beginning . . . At that point we still believed that we, the French, would remain at a distance from it all.

The first few times he was sent out there, he didn't realize the gravity of the situation.

All I ask is that when we get to Spain, they give us the cushy missions and don't mistake us for an enemy cargo ship and fire on us.

He sent us news, with photographs of the country that was already consumed by flames and bloodshed, like the picture of the Spanish nationalist battlecruiser *Canarias* that he'd taken

during a storm. He was proud to show us that he was at the
heart of what was happening.

> *On our way home from Spain we brought a cinematographer
> to film the squadron's manoeuvres, and if you see it on the
> newsreel you can say that it was filmed on 1 March on board
> the torpedo ship. You might even spot me. I set it up so that
> my face appears right opposite the torpedo boat tubes.*

Things rapidly began to escalate as international political
pressure was ratcheted up. His letter of 6 March 1938 was the
first one clearly tinged with anxiety.

> *On Thursday 4 March we left Toulon for wretched Spain
> again. I witnessed the bombardment of Barcelona between 4
> and 6 p.m. and it was awful to see. How they're suffering,
> the Spanish. They want for absolutely everything, bread,
> soap, cigarettes . . . One packet costs the same as 5 kg of
> oranges. A packet of Gauloises goes for 25 pesetas, which is
> the equivalent of 12½ francs.*

That was the year, towards the end of 1938, when it became
increasingly rare for him to be sent home on leave. His letters
took an age to reach us, and sometimes didn't arrive at all.
Spain was divided in two and the post often went astray.

After that, whenever he was home on leave, he wasn't the
same. It was as if he had finally realized it wasn't a game. Then
he would set off again, and I was powerless to do anything. I
couldn't keep him safe and warm inside my belly while we
waited for it all to be over.

He's dead now, and I will never forgive Lucien for that.
Guillaume should never have enlisted, he was far too young.
The navy didn't want him in 1936; he had to get permission
from his parents. Which Lucien should never have given.

Guillaume wanted to see the world. He had always dreamed
of travelling and the navy seemed to offer the easiest way to

achieve that. I didn't want to stop him, I just wanted him to give himself time to grow up and to really think about such a momentous decision. He nagged us and threatened us, but we held our ground. For weeks and weeks every conversation returned to the same subject, with no let-up. And we never gave in.

"I want to travel while I'm young. Later on I'll want to start a family. I'll come back to work for Father in the factory, and to take care of you both when you're old. But now I want to see the world, to find out what it looks like, or I'll always regret it – and that's not my destiny, I know it."

I can still picture him standing in front of me. He was always very tall for his age. When he was sixteen, he looked twenty. There he stood, so sure of himself, so sure of his decision. So different to his friends . . . Étienne, for example, he's twenty now, and still growing. Anyway, Lucien and I formed a united front to prevent Guillaume from doing something stupid. After all, if he enlisted, he would be committing five years of his life – five of his best years – to the navy. The very years when dreams are made, when they are so numerous that they pile up in a great heap and assume the shape of the world.

The Great War had deprived us of all our options, stolen our youth. We woke up exhausted in the aftermath of the immeasurable catastrophe that had left the world bitter, impoverished and devastated.

Lucien knew perfectly well what it meant to be in the army. He knew it meant giving up his youth, his carefree view of life. To begin with, like me, he tried to do everything to dissuade Guillaume. And then – I never understood why or how – the wind changed.

One evening Guillaume came and stood triumphantly before me, waving a letter signed by his father. "I'm leaving tomorrow. You'll be so proud of the man I'm going to become, Mother. You'll see!"

Lucien was behind him, slumped rather than sitting in an armchair.

"Thank you, Father," Guillaume said. Lucien didn't lift his head, didn't throw a single glance in my direction. I could see he felt terrible. I didn't understand why he'd changed his mind. How could he? He had gone through that very same hell – how could he have accepted it for his own son, the flesh of his flesh?

I have never experienced war from the inside.

I have never killed with my own hands. I have never wrestled another person in the mud. And yet I know war. It lays waste to everything that stands in its way. It makes no distinction when it comes to age, nationality, or the greatness of a person's spirit.

War has taken so much from me already that I know it will not stop here. It will not leave me in peace until my heart has been reduced to a pile of ashes and I am forced to continue living in spite of my suffering.

The last war stole my parents, my sister and part of Lucien's soul; every night he relives the horror of the trenches, his breath ragged, his body sweating, his eyes bloodshot, convinced that this time he will not escape the rifle pointed at his chest, horrified at what he had to do to return home alive.

He has forced himself, since his return over twenty years ago, to live with the unsayable; if he spoke about it out loud, I would no longer love him. That is what he told me the day he returned from the front.

People imagine that returning home from war is joyous. They imagine that those days mean the promise of an end to danger, that their lives will be peaceful and tranquil for evermore. But in reality, these days are long winters of buried secrets.

I can still picture Lucien standing in the very spot where my son's comrade was standing now. He came towards me and threw himself at my feet, holding me as tight as he could, and hid his face, which was streaming with tears, in my skirts. He wasn't disfigured like some of the wounded soldiers I had seen returning early from the front. He still walked like the man I had fallen in love with, but something in his expression had been extinguished.

I knew from his face that I could neither celebrate, nor embrace him as I had dreamed of doing for so long. We celebrated the day of our reunion with tears. I saw him cry for the first and only time in my life. He cried like a baby and simply whispered between two strangled sobs: "Don't ever ask me to tell you. I will never tell you, because I can't bear to lose you."

He's never been the same since. The war buried him alive, and not a day has passed since his return when I haven't had to bite my tongue in order not to break the promise that I made him.

I've endured that silence because I didn't want to hear anything more about it, that hateful war. I liked the idea that I would never do it the courtesy of listening to a single word.

And now it had all begun again.

Felix handed us a letter. He insisted on giving it to us in person because he thought so highly of his friend, Guillaume, he told us. His hand was trembling. He seemed so young – like my son. To die so young, at only just twenty-one, it made no sense; it was an outrage, an obscenity.

La Railleuse, *1 May 1940*
Captain Hourcade

> *Mr and Mrs Straub*
> *AMIENS*

Dear Sir and Madam,
   Please find enclosed a letter to your son that reached La Railleuse *but which unfortunately he did not receive.*
   Please accept once more my sincere condolences.
   PS. I have enclosed the ribbon of La Railleuse.

I let the enclosed envelope fall to the floor. It was from me; I had written and posted it two weeks earlier. I took the ribbon and stroked it lightly between my fingers. I held it to my lips, trying to detect his smell and the damp trace of bitter tears.

How is it possible that I have not died of grief? How will I survive the rage that consumes me?

The aftershocks just keep on coming. Why doesn't the earth just open up and swallow me? In the early days of May 1940 my beloved son was supposed to be home on leave for at least two weeks, according to his last letter. We had been expecting him to arrive at any moment. It had been a little while since we'd heard from him, but what with the war and his endless transfers between Toulon, Casablanca, Bizerte, Dakar and Tripoli, not to mention the classified missions we were not allowed to know about, his letters were frequently delayed.

I had fattened the rabbit to make terrines for Guillaume, picked plums and cherries for jam. When I saw this young man push open the garden gate, I was gathering his favourite fruits for the tarts and pies I was planning to make.

It was the season for gooseberries, the fruit he loved most.

The previous year he had missed them, because, after war had been declared in September 1939, he was granted home leave less and less often. We hadn't seen him in over a year, not since January 1939.

Save me some gooseberries this year – I don't want Liliane to gobble them all up this time!

He and his sister squabbled a lot, but they loved each other. She was always spoiling for a fight with her big brother, but it was only to get him to notice her.

I took a step backwards and dropped the basket of gooseberries. The sight of them was unbearable. "He's never going to taste them again," I thought.

It was hardly this young man's fault, but as I looked at him, I couldn't help thinking of my son, who had just been getting on with his life in the certainty that it would last forever. The navy had been given the job of destroying this faith in the future, as if it wasn't sure he was entitled to one.

May God forgive me, but the young sailor who stood before

me, who must have endured so much himself – the fear, the trepidation, the bombardments, the loss of his comrades, in whose place he might perhaps have been – how I hated him, how I hated him with every bone in my body, how I wished it was he who had died instead of my little boy. So that Guillaume would come home and all this madness that men inflict upon each other would finally be at an end.

Felix, 1940

I felt like the lowest of the low. I was ashamed to be me, standing before this survivor who'd managed to do the one thing that the rest of us will undoubtedly fail to do: return. I could see it right away. Not that he mentioned the Great War; you could just see he wasn't the type to shit his pants, and let's face it, the only good reason to desert is fear. He was exactly the type who'd fight to defend his honour, and the honour of his country, too. I, on the other hand, find that the better things are going, the less I care about the fatherland. Especially since I'm sure it firmly intends to send me home feet first.

It was quite something to be standing in front of this woman, so tall and upright; like a queen she was, the kind of lady who never stumbles, even if she's a bit tipsy.

Guillaume had described her perfectly: quite daunting, but with a kind expression. She looked like she could see right through you, like you were made of rice paper. Right away I wished I looked like someone who dreamed big, someone who harboured some great mystery in the depths of my soul, but it's hard to pull off, that kind of thing.

Guillaume was like that too. And when he started talking to you, and laughing, you'd find that for a little while you could think about something other than the misery burning inside us all.

He was tall, with a strong jaw, a penetrating gaze and a wide forehead that was full of ideas. He liked doing gymnastics in the morning; "It makes your clothes hang better," he always said. But the most striking thing about him was his smile. The way it would suddenly change from wolfish to kittenish. You just had to go out with him and all the girls would stare at us. He could have the pick of whoever he wanted. He didn't need to fret about whether his charm would work or not.

I had plenty of time to mull all this over on his parents' front step. At last they invited me in.

It was like a blanket of lead had been draped around his mother's shoulders, and though she was managing to stay dignified, you could sense she was about to collapse.

I wasn't very keen to witness all this grief. It's a private thing. I was a stranger, and it was hard enough dealing with my own.

To top it all, I suddenly found myself shivering, despite the spring sunshine. But I felt it was my duty to stay a bit; to talk to them, listen to them. Tell them some nice stories about their son; make them sad, but not unbearably so.

Guillaume's father invited me to take the most comfortable armchair in the living room and his mother brought me a cup of coffee and a slice of plum tart. I didn't say no. I couldn't.

They didn't eat, and I completely understood why: news like that kills your appetite. When the silence became too much, I looked at the books on the shelves behind Guillaume's father. His head was lowered, and he was staring at his feet.

Now I'm no connoisseur of literature, but Guillaume, all he did was read, read, read, and now I got it. Joseph Conrad, Christopher Columbus, La Pérouse, Louis-Antoine de Bougainville, Jules Verne . . . Books that take you on a journey, tales of adventurers. Now I understood where he'd picked up all his big ideas about the world and about life. His parents had set quite an example. They were upstanding and respectable; they weren't the kind to put stupid ideas in your head, make you feel like you were the one who was all wrong then throw you out of the house.

So I sat in their lounge making polite conversation, going to such lengths to dig up cheerful, happy memories for them that I ended up making him sound like a saint. But there are things you mustn't reveal about the lives of sailors. So I told them nice little stories; I wanted to emphasize that he was the kind of guy who really shouldn't have copped it that night.

There wasn't a lot else to say, really. But it was terrible, the effort I was making to try and fill the hole Guillaume's death had left in their lives.

They were so devastated they couldn't even look at each other, Guillaume's folks. Hélène was despair personified, like a bottomless well of sadness that had just opened up. Lucien looked shaken. Not confused, exactly, but as though there was something gnawing at him . . . I thought they'd at least comfort each other a bit. But maybe that would come later, when they were alone.

Meanwhile I kept talking. I hadn't planned to go so overboard talking about how he'd spent his final hours – it wasn't like it was going to bring him back – so I don't know what made me keep jabbering on. Maybe it was the way they were looking at me, as if I knew something that might change this awful hand that fate had dealt them. Or maybe it was just to fill the silence. And then all of a sudden my head was filled with anger, making me want to behave differently to how I intended . . . it was as though my head was swelling, throbbing. I had to keep talking, talking, and when I get going . . .

As long as they didn't ask me too many awkward questions, it would be all right.

Lucien, 1940

I cannot say anything, obviously. I've kept quiet for so long.
But since my little boy, my little Guillaume, left, the nightmares
that used to haunt me constantly have been replaced by other,
much worse ones. Never would I have imagined that that was
possible. Have I not suffered enough already? Who would have
thought I'd still be paying the price for going to war, over and
over again.

If I had ever imagined that one day I would be tormented by
even worse pain, I would have killed myself. Of course, that would
have been the only thing that would have stopped Guillaume
leaving, kept him from experiencing the same senseless devastation that I had known. Days, weeks, months thinking I was going
to die in the mud, secretly wishing, when a comrade died, that
it had been me instead, for the hope of getting out alive is crueller
than death itself.

I should have killed myself. But I had prayed so hard not
to die that death continued to refuse me its peaceful embrace.

In Guillaume's letters home, the frivolous descriptions of his
time in Toulon had soon been replaced first by nervous antici-
pation about the reality of life in the navy, then resignation
after war was declared, not so long before he died. He was
stationed on a torpedo ship moored in the port of Casablanca.
We ourselves received the news of the outbreak of war like
a thunderbolt. The socialist newspaper *Le Populaire*, dated
2 September 1939, put an end to long weeks of suspense:

Alas, there has only ever been one question. Does Hitler want peace, or at least does he not want war? The world has its answer now: since yesterday morning, German bombs have been falling on Warsaw and other open Polish cities; blood is flowing, destruction, death!

Guillaume had been telling us less and less about his life. It dawned on me that he was no longer allowed to tell us everything. Sometimes his letters were postmarked from an "unknown location". I knew what that meant. Danger. Missions that have only two possible outcomes: success or death.

Sometimes he permitted himself a comment on the international political situation, calling Daladier "Chamberlain's puppet", or criticizing Roosevelt for agreeing to a ceasefire which would simply postpone the conflict for a few years.

I'm sacrificing the best years of my life to this nonsense, but here we are, and we shall have to see it through. They must understand, Hitler and Mussolini, that if they try to attack us, they'll get their arses kicked big time! It's up to us, the younger generation, to fight! Anyway, it'll all be over soon. I'll say it again, Father: it's better that we sort it out now than find ourselves starting it up all over again in ten years' time. In ten years I'll have a nice little house with a proper garden, I'll be happily married to a woman who'll give me beautiful children. I'll be happy, won't I, Father?

My son also expressed concern for me in his last letters home: he was afraid that I might have to go through it all again. The loss of life in "the war to end all wars" had been so great that people were saying that everyone was going to be called up. And that we, the veterans of the last war, would have to return to the front.

I'd have been happy to go, if it had meant that he would not have died. How I wish it was me who had died instead of him.

Not long before, it was me who had been reassuring him, repeating the same old nonsense we'd told ourselves in 1914. "The war will soon be over. We'll be done with the Krauts once and for all. If they didn't get the message in 1918, they will this time. They're bad losers; they just need a little reminder."

How sick I felt to think that he might have the same bad luck. Good God! We were on the wrong side again. On the side of those on the front line. Not on the side of the pen-pushers or the officers.

It was the same in 1916, by the Marne river. We were left all alone, bloody fools, freezing in the trenches, scared shitless, like little kids. If we'd jumped out to relieve ourselves, they would have shot us like rabbits. It was better to stink than to die, considering that death is the worst smell of all.

It was all around us, that sickly sweet odour that makes you want to vomit; it haunted me then and it haunts me now. My God, how did we ever feel hungry again?

Guillaume knew what a farce it was, but enlisted anyway. Not like the other lads his age. They'd never stopped hearing about the courage of those who made it home alive from the Great War. The youngsters of that generation grew up hearing about our exploits, though we never talked about them. They were raised with the idea that you had to be part of that dirty great con trick that is the army if you want to become a man.

I did my best to talk about it differently with Guillaume and Lili. It was inconceivable to me that my children should grow up believing that war embodies noble values. It was all a web of lies; I'd figured that out pretty quickly. What I wanted was that they should understand that conflicts between countries had to be avoided at all costs; they had nothing to do with us. Guillaume knew that, he knew what a farce it was, but he enlisted anyway. He signed up in 1936 for five years. He would have been out by 1941.

And then, with terrible bad luck, war broke out. It really was ill-fated – he only had another year and a half to get through.

What stupidity! What tragedy! You only have to see this lad

standing here now, trembling so hard he's about to spill his coffee, telling us all these silly stories about Guillaume. He's terrified to let slip whatever it is he has been told he's not allowed to say. He's still practically a kid, who had to be propelled through the gates of hell to learn to be a man. Just like me, twenty years ago.

I learned to be a man as I wept with exhaustion in the tunnels we had dug deep under the ground to protect ourselves from the shells that could have buried us alive under showers of blood and mud. I learned to be a man when I began to fear rats and vermin in my sleep. I learned to be a man when I cared more about dying than living. I learned to be a man when I understood there was no such thing as the romantic grandeur of war, that it was a load of lies they spouted to give us poor fools at the front courage. We were being decimated as the generals who decided our fate sat and stuffed their faces, while we lived off rats and stagnant water.

Deep down, whatever this Felix has come to tell us, it's nothing I don't know already. The agony, the horror, there are no words for it . . . fear, death, nights when we shat ourselves with terror, calling for our mothers to make it stop. It's not the kind of thing that looks good written down – we'll be accused of being gutless cowards. At least we were brave enough to stay on our feet. That alone is courage, and heroism. Ah, how the army loves to spout these big words!

But we weren't really brave. Like they say, courage is doing something you don't have the balls for. It wasn't that we were brave in the trenches; we simply had no choice. Once we reached the front, we had shelling ahead and the generals' machine guns pointing at our backsides, just in case anyone was inclined to change his mind. We didn't have the luxury of retreating or even hesitating. Life had trapped us like miserable galley slaves, and we had no choice but to endure the terrible bloodbath to the bitter end. Shells pounding the vast open-air cemetery. Sprays of mud burying the bodies then uncovering them at the next salvo. Bad luck, a bad hand, a losing wicket – and eventually the dreadful day arrives, in spite of all your prayers, when you find yourself in the wrong place at the wrong time.

If only we'd had the choice not to be damned!

All the stories Felix told us – their only purpose was to hollow out a vast grave for us to fill with tears.

He told us everything he could, but I doubt there was anything very new. He focused a bit too much on the good times, the countries they'd been to – Senegal, Spain, Morocco, Algeria, Lebanon, Yugoslavia, Italy . . .

He talked about the coconuts Guillaume used to like to send us, because they keep for eight months or more (in fact we hadn't even got round to tasting them). And the stalls in the medinas of Tangiers, Casablanca, Oran and Bizerte, where Guillaume bought us souvenirs: cards, photographs, teapots, djellabas, babouches.

"You got the djellabas he bought you in Casablanca? What a wag! That was typical of Guillaume. It'd never have occurred to me to send my parents an outfit like that! And he was bloody brave. Everyone looked up to him. Did he ever tell you about the python in Dakar? He hoisted himself right up to the top of a palm tree to get it down. Dakar, what a place . . . Amazing weather, for starters – about 52°C. And just to give you an idea, it's a brutal place, all savannah and rainforest. There's bananas, coconuts and pineapples, and a load of terrifying animals: snakes, leopards, buffalo, vultures, coyotes, jaguars . . ."

I remembered the story of the python. Guillaume had sent us photographs of himself proudly holding the gigantic reptile in his arms. He had done it for a bet, and won the respect of all the other sailors on the ship. We saw the admiration in Felix's eyes, an admiration all the boys must have shared. But none of that would bring my son back.

I suspected that Felix was talking so fast to fill the silence with stories that didn't really belong to him any more.

And as I read the captain's letter, I couldn't help wondering about this young man in front of me – where had Felix been when the ship was hit?

I broke my silence and decided to ask him directly: "Where was the captain? And you – where were you? How did you make it out alive? Tell me everything. I want to know how it happened."

By the way he didn't answer, the way he flushed and fidgeted with discomfort, I could see he was hiding something from us. I'd had it with secrets. Mine kept me from breathing and sleeping at night.

The last time I'd had to face up to a secret was with my son, back in 1936. I had never seen anyone look at me with so much hatred.

I know everything. Sign this damn piece of paper or it'll all come out . . .

He had me. My son had me. I'd never have imagined him capable of blackmail, but he'd been planning it for weeks, it seemed. We shared a secret, and now he was using it against me to gain his freedom.

But I was the one to blame. He was so like me, especially when it came to his interest in women. But he wasn't motivated by despair, like I was. While I needed women in order to forget, as a distraction from my nightmares, he had yet to reach that point. For him, women were about the discovery of a whole new world. How I envied him his enthusiastic self-assurance.

Even as a boy he'd shown an interest in the opposite sex. He collected photographs of naked women from faraway countries. I have to admit that made me smile. I knew that part of his desire to travel was to do with his appetite for the sensual, which he wanted to satisfy before he wed Ginette. However much he loved her, he wanted to discover all that life had to offer before taking the plunge – and no doubt he also wanted to be an experienced lover for her.

He didn't share her typically girlish romantic vision, the idea of giving oneself to a single person, going through life hand in hand. He freely confided his secrets and desires. He never shied away from talking about things that even the bravest men bury deep inside, even things that might be considered shameful.

We had lengthy discussions and I was privy to secrets about his early experiences, which I never disclosed to his mother. I answered all his questions about love: how to seduce a girl; how to facilitate a cure for the clap; how to conceal his romantic escapades from Ginette.

I tried to keep things light when I talked to him; he was such a fast learner. His maturity stood out a mile. He was so far ahead of other young men of his age, who were still struggling to lose their virginity.

The day he discovered my secret, everything changed. Our close relationship, our intimate conversations, it was all over. For several months the only words he addressed to me were defiant.

"I'm going to steal all your women, you'll see," he spat at me one day.

It seems that in this life there is always an ever greater price to pay.

Felix, 1940

Guillaume was a great bloke. He never should've copped it that day.

I sensed the calamity ahead, but somehow I managed to sidestep it. I'd been going on to his folks about all the beautiful places we'd seen, our friendship, how brave he was. I had an actual stomach ache from trying not to trip up . . . Because all the time I was rabbiting on, I was getting more and more caught up in the memories I'd sworn not to reveal. It was all about to come pouring out. The effort I was making to keep it in was exhausting . . . I was fighting against myself. It was a terrible situation to be in, but it wasn't often I managed to keep my trap shut when I needed to.

The truth is, I didn't know much about Guillaume except what he'd chosen to tell me. He was a bit of a mystery, really; he could be damn secretive. It made him seem rather sophisticated, actually. I'd never met anyone who knew how to stop talking just before he said too much, the way he did.

I'm the absolute opposite, a real big mouth. I didn't mind until I met him. I thought, well, that's just what I'm like. I'm never going to change the way I am. But then something happened that really made me think. I was out on shore leave with Guillaume the Great – that's what we called him because not only was he not a big mouth even though he really knew how to talk, but he was also extremely tall, even though he didn't make a big deal of it. Basically the complete opposite of me. The complete opposite of most of us, I'd say.

Anyway, as soon as we went ashore the girls would start throwing themselves at him. He made it look so easy to try his luck with some pretty lass. He might as well have been a prince!

You should have seen them: all starry-eyed, simpering and flirting like he was the last man on earth. We were all so envious of him! We'd sit round the table fidgeting with our beers while he'd be chatting up some young lady. We were acting like we didn't care, but in reality we were tied up in knots. Even though we wouldn't have admitted it for the world, we were dying of jealousy. Going out with him was like slamming the door on any hope we might ever have had of landing a girl.

If I had my eye on some bird, I had to make a real effort – pretend that I was even keener than I was, really try hard. I'd have to risk being given the brush-off – more than once, maybe – as though that was expected because even the Queen of England paled in comparison to her, and then move on to flowers, serenades . . .

But whatever Guillaume had was so powerful that for him it was the opposite. He'd just look all offhand and it was in the bag. Picking up a girl was easy as pie for him, sickeningly so. I'd watch him do it: he'd walk into a room, catch the eye of the one he liked the look of most – and it was always the most attractive one, obviously; the one we all fancied too . . . That was the thing. We'd get the leftovers after he took the lion's share.

And then the incredible thing was that after that he'd just ignore her. He'd sit drinking, singing, larking about with the rest of us, throwing down a few coins for a tip. I don't know if it was all an act, but in any case, he never looked over at her once.

She'd have no idea what to do to get his attention. All the other lads would be trying it on with her but she'd give them all the brush-off. She just wouldn't get it. She'd sit there moping, clearly thinking, What did I do? Why doesn't he like me any more? It was incredible. You had to take your hat off to him, give him a round of applause as though he'd performed a magic trick, because it always worked – she'd always crack. She'd have to risk it. And so they always came to him, all without him lifting a finger. All he had to do now was bend down to kiss her.

It never looked like he'd planned it that way, though. It was an impressive way to snare his prey.

We'd always laugh, but it was never quite as genuine as it sounded, because our pride was wounded. After a performance like that you'd need a bit of confidence to get back on the saddle, stop yourself thinking it wasn't even worth having a go.

That was all we talked about. Girls, I mean. Because if there's one thing that preoccupies a sailor at sea, it's women. I'm a bit ashamed to admit it, but the one thing that kept me going on the voyage from Casablanca to here was the thought of meeting Guillaume's sister, Liliane. She was only seventeen and I was twenty-four. I'd seen her picture. She was definitely worth the journey on her own. I used to beg him, "Let me write to her, Guillaume! Go on, be a pal!" He never gave in, the bastard. Every time he'd say, "Oh no. Not before you've had a go with one of my conquests first!"

I can't bear to think of that now. To think that after all that, he's not even here to stop me from doing anything now. That I still have the chance to chat up girls, even in the midst of all this sadness. But it's just that I'm going back there, and there's no one waiting for me at home. Who's going to worry about me when the ship's caught in waves as high as a house? No one! Who'll be praying to see me again, after a lucky escape from an enemy torpedo? No one!

Guillaume must have had someone waiting for him, because he never seemed to worry about that sort of thing. But it's hard to be sure, because he never talked about it.

Luckily, I had the presence of mind not to bring all this up in front of his parents – all his love affairs, I mean. Not because it's shameful, but I'm sure my mate wouldn't have wanted me to tell his old ma about that stuff. And even if he had got a girl or two up the duff, he wouldn't be the first or the last not to face the music. And at least he had a damned good excuse . . .

But Guillaume wasn't as stupid as some of the others. He knew how to be careful. God damn it, not that it matters any more. No one will ever know, now he's gone.

I have to say we didn't hold back, especially in Casablanca. When I think about those evenings and nights in Bousbir . . . There were quite a few of us who weren't interested in being tourists; Bousbir was the only part of town we knew. Everything you needed was there, so there was no need to go anywhere else. We knew our way around, and that's where we spent our leave and our pay. During the day there were barbers for the men, hairdressers for the ladies, a tobacconist, cafés, restaurants, boutiques, a hammam, a cinema and a stall selling doughnuts. At night everything changed; there was a different atmosphere. It was so busy, so bustling, you could forget about your worries till the morning. The tobacco seller made his night's takings even before the first stars appeared; all he had to do was move in on the hawkers lurking in shadowy corners.

Then Guillaume and I would go and settle ourselves in one of our favourite cafés. Either the Qahwa Dial el Qsub or the Café des Roseaux for its dope and its liquor . . . The Café du Raïs for its atmosphere, with musicians from the Atlas Mountains who played the *tarija* and the *gita* all night long, eyes closed, imagining themselves going home to their oases. But Guillaume swore by the Cinema Café, because when he was down in the dumps that was the only place that could cheer him up. Or we might go and see a film at the fleapit in Bousbir. It was more down to earth, not like being with the fancy bourgeois folk at the other cinemas. You didn't need to feel self-conscious about what you were wearing or how you talked. We saw a lot of Egyptian flicks there. There were European ones too, but not every evening. Watching Guillaume watch a film was a spectacle in itself – his absolute concentration on the lines and the ideas, like he didn't want to forget a thing. In an especially thrilling scene, he'd repeat his favourite lines under his breath. Afterwards we'd have a beer, play a hand of *ronda*, smoke some dope. If the film was really good, Guillaume would ignore the Bousbir ladies, even the pretty ones. They'd show their legs and wave their hennaed hands at him, try to lure him with their kohl-rimmed eyes, or make

promises with their red-painted lips, whistling at him all the
words of Arabic we knew, "*T'ala t'alleq m'aya*", meaning "Are
we going to go to bed together?" But he'd be otherwise preoccupied. And I think the truth was he preferred to chase than
be chased, and paying for sex wasn't really his thing.

I wasn't always careful when it came to women, I have to
admit. The number of times I picked up the clap – my God,
when your manhood looks like it's about to fall to bits . . . That
reminds me of Gaston – once he got back really late after a
night out in Bousbir and he was absolutely wild, hopping from
one foot to the other, unable to contain himself. The way he
was squirming, his hands down his trousers, he didn't have to
spell it out. "Shit, boys, shit, oh my God, she kept on saying,
berd n bula, berd n bula, berd n bula." The rest of us didn't
know what he was on about, but Guillaume shot back: "That's
easy, that one, Gaston. Now you know how to say 'gonorrhoea'
in Arabic!"

During the dark moments, when it felt like things were falling
apart, it was always Guillaume we'd go and talk to. He always
knew what to do. You'd think he'd heard it all before. He was
younger than us, but so much more bloody self-assured.

All these tales of prostitutes, dope and the clap, it wasn't the
kind of thing you'd tell his parents', even if it was only to say
that he was classier than all that. I imagine I wouldn't want my
pal Jeannot to show up at my parents, trying to find something
nice to say about me, and only managing to think of the time
I ended up with some whore in a brothel, so plastered that I
had no idea what tricks I'd paid her to turn.

Put like that it sounds sordid. But we were making the most
of life. Gulping down great draughts of it, because who knew,
that time could be our last. It was a way of giving the finger
to fate, a balm for our wounds and for the friends we'd already
lost. We were brothers now, the most precious things in each
other's lives.

But I was keeping all this to myself as much as I could,
because his folks wouldn't get it. And also because it was

Guillaume's last chance to make a good impression. After this, it would all be over as far as he was concerned . . . I kept saying to myself, "Felix, get it over with, don't hang about; you know what you're like, you're going to let something slip in a minute. You never know when to stop and it's bound to end in tears." I couldn't help myself. My chin was trembling with emotion at all the memories that were pouring out as I talked about him. As I said, Guillaume was the strong, silent type. Never talked unless he needed to. I should try and be like him, but I can't. The more I hold things in, the more they feel like they're about to burst out. And that was exactly what was going to happen here, but I managed to restrain myself. I said lots of touching things about their son, the kind of memories that parents want to hear. Actually, I did pretty well. But that's exactly my problem: as soon as I gain confidence, I keep going and don't know when to stop.

He was a great bloke, Guillaume, it's such rotten luck . . . I kept repeating that, but it was like there was something burning my lips, and his father started asking all these questions.

"And you, where were you?"

"Well, it's true that it should have been me on the ship."

They both froze.

His mother, stiff as a post, put her coffee cup down on the saucer. I couldn't look at them, I felt such a fool. I'd been categorically caught out.

"What do you mean?" they asked. Obviously, that was the logical question. Not that logic was my strong point, clearly.

His sister Liliane chose the precise moment of my humiliation to walk into the room. To make matters worse, she was even prettier than in the photographs. There was rage in her eyes and I understood that I'd made a hash of it with her as well, before I'd even begun.

I had no other choice but to explain to them that what had happened to Guillaume was even more unfair than they'd first thought.

War, life, it's all the epitome of injustice. Justice is a nice idea that becomes a dirty word the minute you find yourself on the front line. It's always the people giving the orders who talk about justice, with their arses wedged into their nice plush armchairs, Cuban cigars hanging out of their gobs, all those veterans sent to their deaths on their consciences – justice is always on their side, and their job is to make sure it stays that way.

I had questions too. Guillaume never wanted to tell us how he'd managed to enlist in the navy even though he was under-age. He was in a hurry to see the world . . . only to die at the age of twenty-one. He was in such a hurry to get ahead of us all. What appalling luck. But life's a game of roulette . . . You win some, you lose some. And there are some people who, even if they've been dealt a good hand at the start, and they go all in with their eyes closed, are destined to live a life as fleeting as a shooting star.

Loubna, 2005

I've always thought there's no such thing as coincidence. Especially when you don't make space for it. When I answered the phone this morning, I had the strong feeling that something was about to change, that today was going to be a turning point in my life.

"Are you still dreaming of having your own cinema? Come over this evening after work, say one thirty – okay?" It was the irresistible and very American accent of Liz, a New York-born friend whom I've been hanging out with for the last few months, that woke me up.

Ever since I was a little girl I've been surrounded by artists and friends who are mad about cinema. Liz is one – she owns Rick's Café, on Sour-Jdid Boulevard, just beyond the port. The restaurant is inspired by the café that Rick, the Humphrey Bogart character, runs in *Casablanca*. Upstairs there's a lounge where punters can watch *Casablanca* on a loop, over cigars and whisky. On evenings when I feel like a chat, or simply someone to hang out with who I feel close to, I pop by to see her.

After the last customers, kitchen staff and waiters have gone, she locks up and takes down her best bottle of cognac. I'll often bring along one of my latest cinematic discoveries and interrupt Rick and Ilsa's dialogue.

But in any case those two really weren't destined to love each other in this world. Like my parents and my father's parents.

I'd told Liz about my project. Unsurprisingly, given that she'd opened a restaurant paying homage to one of the best-known films in the history of cinema, she'd been immediately charmed by the idea. What I didn't know was that she had been quietly working behind the scenes to help it come to fruition.

It was 1.30 a.m. precisely when she opened the door to me. There was a gentle breeze in the air, and the voices of passers-by echoed around the little square, which was set back from the boulevard and adjoined the walls of the old medina.

Beckoning me inside with a whisper, she drew me aside on the patio before pushing open the heavy, ruby-red velvet curtains.

"He's interested in your cinema idea. But I'm warning you, he's dangerous."

I wasn't happy that she'd landed me in this uncomfortable situation. Her all-American enthusiasm sometimes pushed her to charge headlong into situations while ignoring the potential risks. I suspected she believed she had a guardian angel that meant she'd always be able to extricate herself from any kind of confrontation, but I was far from sharing this belief, which wasn't surprising given the legacy I'd been left by my absent forebears. I wanted my cinema, but not at any price.

"What do you mean, dangerous? Come on Liz, seriously! You don't mess around with the mafia here. I don't need that and nor do you."

She snorted with laughter and slapped her hand over my mouth to stop me saying any more. Her delighted expression made her look childishly pleased with herself.

"Don't be an idiot! I'm not saying another word – you'll figure it out on your own."

She took me upstairs to the lounge. All the lights had been turned off. The riad, lit entirely by candles in wrought-iron holders sitting on the empty tables, was filled with an atmosphere of mystery. My heart was beating fast and loud, as though it might burst out of my chest. Liz was being so mysterious that I couldn't help quickening my pace, even though I wanted nothing more than to hide beneath a tablecloth.

From a corner of the lounge, wreaths of cigar smoke perfumed the air, and I glimpsed ice cubes glinting in a large glass. Liz was clearly charmed by her guest's elegant ways. For her, luxury isn't ostentation but refinement. If you have to smoke, then it must be the best cigars, Romeo y Julieta, Cohiba or Montecristo, which she imported from Cuba, where she'd once lived for several months with a man called Castro: "Great nephew or cousin, I could never quite figure out which." The same applied to whisky, rum, cognac and wine, as well as spices, tea, coffee and chocolate.

I smelled the aftershave of the unknown investor even before I saw him. He shared my taste for old-fashioned elegance.

Liz walked ahead of me and introduced me to the man from whom emanated an intoxicating aroma of cigar smoke, honey-coloured liquor and leather.

He stood and shook my hand.

"*Enchanté*. I am Ali."

He held my hand in his a second too long and gave me a look that was just a touch too intense. I immediately understood what Liz meant. Ali Basri is dangerously irresistible. And for good reason. I know about him. Everyone does. The things I know about him are the things that any Moroccan knows who's ever picked up a copy of *Huffington Post Maghreb*. He's not only one of the wealthiest men in the country but its most high-profile bachelor, and his reputation as a ruthless player in the world of finance is firmly established.

I sat down opposite Ali. He fixed me with his saturnine gaze. He had shining, dark eyes, carefully cultivated three-day stubble, and long, slicked-back hair tied up in a ponytail. I don't usually like long hair on men, but I have to admit it suited him. I imagine everything suits him, to be honest. He was wearing an electric-blue suit and a white shirt. The suit was beautifully cut, the fabric fell perfectly, and the bold colour set off his dark skin superbly well. His appearance was relaxed, confident and elegant. He looked quite at home; the soft lighting and stylish furniture were made for him.

Ali watched me intently while Liz poured me a glass of my favourite cognac. I thought back to the most recent article about him, which, quite by chance, I happened to have read just a few days earlier. The journalist portrayed a meteoric and dazzling career: by the age of thirty he was associating with the wealthiest families from the Emirates. The point of the article was essentially to highlight the altruism of the young billionaire who "is now one of the vital strengths of the kingdom. Morocco is a young country, but it will inevitably grow older and encounter the same difficulties as ageing countries are dealing with today. This is why we have to invest in the young and offer them the keys to the future." The writer went on to explain in detail the project to finance business schools offering short degrees which was being piloted in Casablanca. "All these endless university degrees, it's completely out of date, it's not remotely adapted to young people today. They need to learn to fight for what they want to achieve – very early, very fast, very hard. They have to set up their first business and have gone bankrupt before they're twenty, so they can start again and do it better, fortified by the mistakes they've made." The journalist, who had quite clearly succumbed to his charms, concluded with the undeniably pertinent observation about the correlation between his dazzling success and his dazzling smile, before asking him if he had any advice for a young person just starting out. "Never forget that in business, anything goes!" he'd proclaimed in response.

I tried to dispel the awkwardness I felt as we talked. I couldn't but admire his bearing and his success, and yet at the same time I was furious with myself at how easily I lost my composure. He was extremely attractive, and he knew it. I was flustered, and he knew that too. He was quite used to having that effect on women.

I decided to get straight to the point. After all, this was basically the most important job interview of my life.

"As I think Liz has already told you, I have this plan to open my own cinema. I've got plenty of experience. At the moment I'm working on a week-long programme at the Rialto showcasing women in Middle Eastern film."

I watched his reaction carefully for a few moments. If we

were to work together, or rather if I was to work for him, because it was he who'd be putting in the money, I didn't want to find myself fettered, to lose the glorious freedom that my current boss allowed me. Djamel had never rejected a single one of my programming ideas, not even my Bergman week. Ali looked interested but said nothing. I went on:

"I was thinking of spotlighting Moroccan cinema with Saâd Chraïbi's trilogy, *Women . . . and Women*, *Jail Girl* and *Women in Mirrors*. Or perhaps Nabil Ayouch's *Much Loved*."

"What about Oum Kalthoum?"

I smiled. "We could certainly think about a retrospective of the films she appeared in. We've got the rights, so there wouldn't be any problem."

"What about *Cairo 6.7.8.*, since we're talking about Egyptian films?"

Liz, excited, broke into the conversation.

"I can tell you're both equally passionate about the cinema!"

Ali held my gaze for a few seconds. I saw for a moment a glint of something that I couldn't interpret, something between admiration and challenge.

It was he who broke the silence and, without responding to our hostess, without giving the slightest indication that he was even aware of her presence, he carried on with what was beginning to seem less and less like a job interview.

"I imagine you already have an idea of where you'd like your cinema to be located."

"I do, actually. The idea is to have a cinema that could only be found in Casablanca. Those architectural gems in the art deco style. I'm not thinking of rebuilding the cinema in the United Nations Square that was once the biggest in Africa. My ambition is much more modest than resurrecting the Vox. But I'm very attached to the colonial district. That's where I grew up, near the central market. I've watched the glories of the area fall into ruin over the years: the enormous cinema being knocked down, the Colisée becoming a warehouse. But – and I'm sure as an entrepreneur you're aware of all this – now the fashion is to restore all these old buildings. At long last the centre of Casablanca is taking pride in itself, the buildings there are being developed and renovated rather than left to rot. It's in the Casablancan DNA."

I was feeling more confident now; I'd forgotten my earlier shyness.

"I think Gauthier would be the right part of town for this kind of place."

He nodded in agreement. He was one of those people who'd grown up and still lived in the Anfa Hills and liked to slum it at the cool, edgy places in Gauthier and Maârif.

"Actually, there's one particular house I've got my eye on. An old colonial building. Completely derelict. It's on the corner of a busy boulevard lined with palm trees. There are a couple of bookshops on the road that runs perpendicular to it. I think it's the perfect location."

I took a scrap of paper and a pen out of my bag and sketched an outline of the house.

"The railings are choked with trees, brambles and overgrown grass, but I broke in one night and I could see exactly what I wanted to do."

My voice, without me even being aware of it, was becoming more self-assured, and I was no longer thrown by Ali's unbridled sexual magnetism.

"It's built over three floors. There's a double staircase that has to stay."

Ali leaned forward to look at my sketch more closely.

"In fact, everything has to stay," I went on. "There'd be one screen on the ground floor and another upstairs. New releases downstairs and special programmes upstairs."

"What about the second floor?"

"There's a massive terrace and two small towers up on the roof. I've taken a good look and as far as I can tell one of them could definitely be turned into a projection room."

"But you couldn't have a permanent outdoor screen."

"There's a tall white building next door, at the perfect angle.

It's being used for an advertising hoarding at the moment. So we could have a third screen, open air, just like the one at the Vox in the 1930s. In the summer we could open up the doors to create an evening breeze."

Ali sank into his chair and put his fingers to his lips, lost in thought. I decided to play my trump card.

"And obviously, there's an area that would make a wonderful garden, with an open-air café where people could come for a drink and something to eat before or after the film. It's in the shade of the most stunning, huge bougainvillea that hasn't been touched for decades."

Ali picked up his glass and drained it in one go.

"All right then. I want to see this house."

Liz had been looking sleepy, but now she sat up with a start, alarmed.

"But it's almost three in the morning!"

He didn't reply. He stood up from his chair and looked at me, vaguely irritated that I wasn't in more of a hurry.

When I'd arrived I'd spotted the Maserati parked in front of Rick's Café. Clearly it was his. I ran down the stairs after him. He waved to Liz, who looked relieved that she could finally go to bed and didn't have to go with us to see an abandoned house in the middle of the night.

He sped off, tyres squealing. He drove fast, and there was no one on the streets. For the first time in my entire life I found myself in one of those cars I'd seen when I was a child, roaring down Kennedy Boulevard towards the sea. No longer was I just a bystander, looking at the handsome drivers sporting sunglasses behind tinted windows, focusing more on how they looked than on the road, feigning indifference but in reality acutely conscious of the envy in the eyes of the people watching them pass. They were being observed and they knew it. There was nothing around them that they couldn't possess.

"Let's make the most of this. Shall we go for a spin? I've only just bought it, I'm not bored of it yet."

It was the middle of the night. The streetlamps were dimly

lit and the car gobbled up the kilometres, crossing the city in what seemed like a matter of seconds. We sped down Corniche Boulevard along the ocean. I couldn't smell it, but it was there, a great, dark, silent zone.

Ali drove past the Hassan II mosque, the D'el Hank lighthouse, then followed the road along the Aïn Diab beach. He took the roundabout by the Grand Morocco Mall before doing a U-turn at speed.

At last he slowed down. For the first time he seemed conscious of my presence.

"Where is this house exactly?"

"On the corner of Moussa-ben-Moussaïr Street and Moulay-Youssef Boulevard."

He thought for a moment.

"Oh yes, I know that boulevard. It's not far from the Lycée Lyautey."

He swerved off again, putting his foot down hard on the accelerator, back along Corniche Boulevard, but this time in the opposite direction. He turned right onto Kennedy Boulevard and sped up the road towards the Anfa Hills, then turned onto Franklin-Roosevelt Boulevard, where the crowds of the city are forgotten, and there's an atmosphere a bit like Beverly Hills. Gradually, as we approached the Maârif neighbourhood, we found ourselves back in the urban sprawl over which the brightly lit twin towers loomed, proudly embracing the district where all the moneyed set had to see and be seen.

I didn't need to tell him to take the right fork down Mouhamed Zerktouni Boulevard, then to go down Moussa-ben-Moussaïr Street. He knew the area like the back of his hand. The house was all the way at the end of the street, on the left, just before the turning onto Moulay-Youssef Boulevard.

"I used to go to the café opposite for orange juice. My gym wasn't far, in the Twins. I walked past it afterwards on my way back to work. It meant I didn't always bump into the same people."

He parked. There was no one about apart from us. My ears hummed in the enveloping silence. We stood in front of the house that I'd been dreaming of turning into a cinema since my childhood. He was looking around and sizing up the immediate neighbourhood. He turned to me and said:

"I have to admit that I used to come here because I liked the area. It's quiet. The streets are pretty. There's a sense of space. The tall palm trees growing down the centre of the boulevard give it a lovely atmosphere all year round."

He looked straight at me.

"You're right. It's the perfect spot."

I felt myself blushing. I felt so stupid standing there like a little girl waiting for approval from someone she admired. I didn't know Ali at all. I had no idea if he was a decent person, nor what to think about someone whose motto was "Never forget that in business, anything goes!"

I didn't know if he'd truly earned his place in the spotlight, or if it was family money that had got him where he was. Liz would have told me off, she'd have reminded me with her all-American enthusiasm that there's no such thing as undeserved glory. I know she has a thing for successful businessmen in general and Moroccan ones in particular. A number of them are her friends, regulars at Rick's. She likes their manners, their warmth, and the effortless way they go in for the kill. "Don't deceive yourself, my love! They're just as much bastards as American businessmen, but they have better manners, and as far as I'm concerned that's worth all the money in the world," she said to me one evening. I know that's the world she used to move in when she lived in New York, but she preferred the more relaxed attitude she found here, which left room for laughter.

It remained to be seen precisely what kind of bastard Ali was. While I was pondering this, he took a photograph of the house and seemed to be considering the layout I'd suggested.

"Let's go inside. How did you get in last time?"

It was four thirty in the morning, my eyes were burning

with exhaustion, but Ali was impatiently shaking the iron gates blocking the entrance to the overgrown garden: grass almost two metres high, brambles, trees that hadn't been cut back for years blooming high and wide, looking like they might consume the house itself.

"Behind the bougainvillea there's a gap at the top of the wall. You have to climb up there and then jump over to the other side. It's easy."

He didn't wait for further instructions from me. He dived beneath a thick, flowering branch and, gripping the gate with one hand and using the other one to hold on to the stone wall that encircled the building, he clambered over.

About to follow him, I saw he was holding out his hand to me. He was perched on the wall and holding the branch clear.

After a brief hesitation, I took his hand. He pulled me up to him and I held on to him so as not to lose my balance. He smelled good.

I quickly let go and threw myself down into the high grass. I cleared a path to the front steps. Dawn was breaking. The trees would soon be glowing in the early-morning spring light.

A moment later he had caught up with me by the front door. The cinema that I had dreamed of for so long was taking shape.

Before me – despite the abandoned garden, despite the ruined parapet, despite the once-white Casablanca building, dating from the beginning of the last century, now drab and grey – I saw a marvellous place. And I saw in Ali the undoubt-edly one-off possibility of bringing it back to life.

I could sense the glories that this building had once contained, and tried to imagine it all: the location, the garden, the layout that would allow us to create an unusual cinema with an open-air screening room on the roof, the art deco metalwork along the balconies on the ground floor, the first floor and the roof, the plaster reliefs surrounding the doors and windows, the imposing black and white marble central staircase that opened up on the ground and first floors to vast reception areas, the intact green tiles on the roof of the awning, and the mouldings that curved like the bow of a ship, breaking up the straight lines of the rest of the building.

"It's all perfect – the layout, I mean. Look how beautiful the space is when you come in, how elegant it is. It's the same when you go upstairs. It means we wouldn't have to knock down many interior walls. Obviously, we'd have to block the windows to make a large dark screening room here and upstairs, but that's all."

Ali remained silent, looking around intently.

"The bathrooms upstairs are incredible; the floors are white marble with fine black veins. There's one on the left of the staircase and one on the right, one for men and one for women. And it's all in excellent condition."

I led him up the stairs. The pale morning light flooding in through the window facing us lit up the room. It reflected off the walls, making them glow, its shimmer dissimulating the grime and dust of years of neglect. I showed him the deserted rooms and drew his attention to a frieze of gilded mosaic tiles.

"I just wanted to show you the central area on both floors. A series of interconnecting areas that must have been the office, living room and reception room, with no supporting walls – which is a stroke of luck, right?"

He had barely glanced at me since we'd left Rick's Café, but now he looked me straight in the eye. I noticed in passing that his expression seemed to have changed, but I was carried away by my enthusiasm. I felt completely at home inside this building. Where other people would have seen a ruin to be knocked down, I saw a dazzling picture palace.

"Are you ready for the showpiece?"

Without waiting for an answer, I bounded four steps at a time up the dusty stairs that led to the roof terrace.

Dazed by the sunlight, we took a few moments to get used to the bright rays cast from all directions. We were on an ark, a veranda surrounded by virgin forest, in a bubble of silence in the heart of the city's deafening hubbub. Although I had been to the house on multiple occasions, every time I came up here I found myself entranced, knocked sideways with excitement, my heart thumping. I stood there for a few moments, taking in the view and the atmosphere of this haven of peace before I spoke.

"And those two flat-roofed towers are the perfect place for housing the projection booth when we want to project films on that wall."

He turned round to see what I was pointing to: a large, imposing building, set back a few metres behind the low wall at the back of the house.

I sat down on the ground and beckoned Ali over. I knew it was very impressive at first sight. I was so convinced, I could only hope he would be too.

I carried on rhapsodizing, pointing at the wall that I could already picture showing cinematic masterpieces: how the huge white screen would make the grain of black and white films like those of Orson Welles and Fritz Lang sparkle; how the bleached concrete would show off the luminous complexions of beautiful stars such as Marilyn Monroe, Bette Davis, Arletty, Ingrid Bergman, Faten Hamama, Shadia, Sabah, Sophia Loren . . .

Suddenly it occurred to me that I hadn't heard the sound of his voice since the beginning of my monologue. I stopped talking. While I had been trying to make him feel the magic that we could create by bringing this place to life, he had been watching me the entire time with an intense expression on his face that made me think of the fire beneath the ice.

Hélène, 1940

All these years, it's as though we've been dancing on a volcano. Sometimes it would rumble, portentously, but none of us wanted to pay it any attention. When I think back to Guillaume and Lili's childhood, I see it bathed in a golden glow, which is gone the second my jumbled thoughts return to the present. I cannot bear the thought of the death of my son. I keep returning, over and over again, to a burning memory.

We knew real happiness. Our life was filled with music, the knowledge that we wanted for nothing, a sense of fulfilment, days without fear. As the years passed, the distant echo of dictators and black and white film reels bore witness to terrible things, only making us want even more to enjoy every last drop of our happiness.

Guillaume had always had a gift for joy and a thirst for life, just as I once had, before the war came.

I can see him, as though in fast forward, on each of the rare periods when he was allowed home on leave.

I remember the very last time; he stayed for two weeks. He had been in Bizerte, and he showered us with gifts from the east: orange flower water, djellabas, necklaces for Lili and me, a sabre for his father. Each time he returned he brought stories, photographs and postcards that I arranged in an album. Now that is all I have left of him, and my hands tremble at the thought of his absence.

I close my eyes. I can feel his skin beneath my fingers. When he came home from Brazzaville, I placed fresh poultices on the sunburn on his neck to relieve the pain. If I breathe deeply my bruised memory captures his smell, catches hold of a trace of him. The smell of his hair in the rain, of his hands after he had been swimming and diving for hours in the Channel, when we used to take them to Tréport for the summer holidays. The smell of his cheeks, flushed with his first alcoholic drink. His intense concentration when I showed him the secret of making *pastis*. His imposing figure in the corner of the kitchen as he gobbled up half a plum tart with a mischievous grin, smug at having had more than the others. His vivacious smile when he turned up at the front door for a surprise Christmas visit. An unbroken stream of memories. My eyes are blurry with tears: such lovely memories, so clear it's as if I were reliving them. I see him from behind, standing on the quay. He turns around, touched that we have come to see him in Toulon. Then Lucien puts his hand on my shoulder. Everything vanishes as he takes my son away from me a second time.

I try with all my might to bring those moments back, but I realize that as his years in the navy went by, the more unreal his presence on leave became. At the beginning it would take me a few minutes to recognize his face, then it began to take longer and longer to overcome the sense of unfamiliarity that emanated from him. He was turning into a man, and before his eyes had passed arid sunlight, profound darkness, joy, pain and death. I could see it. He had ghosts imprinted on his face.

The last time I saw my son, he had only a little over a year to go before he finished his tour of duty. He was going to return home to his former life. It felt like an eternity, and I made him promise to come back as often as he could. I told him he would have all the time in the world to enjoy himself and fall in love after he left the navy. The very last time I saw him, he said to me, "Mother, I promise you, I'll be home as soon as I can!"

Felix, 1940

Guillaume absolutely insisted on offering me his shore leave the day of the explosion. Blimey, what was I meant to do? I jumped at the chance! Once the war had started it had been getting harder and harder to get shore leave, so I didn't need to be asked twice . . . It's true it was a bit of an odd thing for him to do. After all, he was no different to the rest of us, he needed a break too, but from my point of view it was a godsend.

You have to realize we were having a hard time and getting fewer and fewer breathers. Except maybe with girls . . . When we went back to Toulon, what with war having been declared, the fear, the threat that was growing and all the rest of it, they were a lot less hoity-toity with us . . . We didn't have to get all dressed up any more. But what do you know, we couldn't enjoy it because we were nailed to the ship. We were going back and forth to Spain – the Spanish were getting it right in the neck now, they really had no chance. And then, every fourth morning, we'd set sail for Tunisia or Algeria. I can't even talk about it.

It definitely looked like Hitler had decided to stir up trouble. Poland didn't mean to let itself be trampled all over, but they couldn't hold out very long, the poor buggers . . . We were a bit naïve to think the Krauts were going take a breather before they helped themselves to Danzig. And look at the disaster that came after . . . Things escalated even further. And bingo, we were off again to Bizerte, Casablanca, we even went all the way to Yugoslavia, then back to Toulon. We had to be ready for anything, day or night, they told us.

We felt a bit far away from the action, since Poland's way

over on the other side of the continent. But we weren't taking it easy, that's for sure.

For us, the disaster began with the *Pluton* – a battlecruiser that, like us, often docked in Casablanca. We'd even escorted it to Algiers in October 1938. It was a massive minelayer used to transport troops. The main thing was it could go really fast, up to thirty knots.

At the start of the war, we'd been warned that the Germans were planning to attack the Moroccan coast. From that moment on, we weren't allowed to let anything slip in our letters home – couldn't say anything about what we were doing or where we were. So we filled them with details of our meals, the weather, any old rubbish really. And as things heated up our letters were taking longer to arrive because they had to check we weren't writing in code.

Our families weren't allowed to know a thing. The official story, of course – what the newspapers said, and what they told the families of people who'd died in their letters from the generals – was that the *Pluton* had suffered damage, something to do with maintenance . . . just like us with *La Railleuse*! Fancy that.

It really pissed me off to listen to this crap and have to go along with it. It was wartime. Did they really want people to believe that we were so stupid as to set out to sea in a game of hide-and-seek with the Krauts without first making sure that everything was in proper working order?

So what I'm about to tell you is top secret . . . The *Pluton* was supposed to counter attacks from German submarines by laying out a defensive field with a hundred mines that had been loaded on board in Brest. They got to Casablanca, docked at the Delure jetty, and waited a week for instructions. All that and then, curiously, it turned out that the Germans hadn't budged; they weren't on their way to the Atlantic coast of Morocco at all. So our colleagues were ordered to appear to be laying mines but to get them off board when they next reached port.

That's when it blew up.

The bridge at the back turned red and huge flames lit up the sky. We weren't far away and we saw it all. Heard it all, more than anything. With the first explosion we knew what had happened. And then it started again right away. The second was dreadful . . . The glass in the portholes on all the nearby ships and in the windows of the cars and buildings in the port was smashed to smithereens. The sea was on fire. It was indescribable, I'm telling you, and I probably sound like a nutter, but the leaking oil was burning like the flames of hell. I've never seen anything like it. In less than an hour, the *Pluton*, a massive ship of 5,000 tons, 100 metres long, had been engulfed by waves like molten lava.

We ran towards it. We could see them thrashing about in the flames . . . The air, the water, the bodies of the living, limbs torn to pieces . . . Everything was on fire, and the ship was slowly being swallowed like it was in quicksand.

These sailors – our friends, our brothers, men we'd gone drinking with in Bousbir – were wrestling with death, but it had already won. The days leading up to the explosion, we'd gone and got drunk together on rosé. But I don't pity them, those poor men. Wherever they are now, at least nothing can hurt them any more.

The ship blew up on 13 September 1939, in Casablanca, a few months before ours did. It was a splendid fireworks display, almost like a celebration of the war that had just been declared. You can't help thinking they were the first people to die in the war. Especially when the official version makes out it was the fault of some halfwit who let two or three hundred poor souls die just because he'd forgotten to defuse a mine.

We were officially forbidden to mention a single word of all this . . . But I owe you the truth, because I'd hope that someone in my place would tell my folks.

Back in Casablanca, none of us believed a word of what we were told. But watch out you if you were thinking about contradicting them, you daft sap of a sailor! Remember your place is to serve your country, thank you very much.

Obviously there were plenty of questions in the days after
the explosion. And obviously all of us couldn't help thinking
it might've been us in their place . . . Because frankly no one
believed for a second the story that it was negligence. What
was the point of this charade? They were pretending to be
laying mines, when actually they were packing them all away,
and then the whole ship blew up?

As far as we could see, there was no doubt about it: there
were informers in Casablanca telling the Krauts our movements. And meanwhile they were all safe and sound, given
they'd managed to stop us installing a defensive line to keep
them from entering, and they even had time to toss a well-
aimed torpedo onto the pile of mines on board the *Pluton* to
put the whole lot out of commission.

Then a few months later it was our ship, *La Railleuse*, that
exploded – all on its own, apparently. "Negligence during
routine maintenance," they said . . . the same story. Twenty-
eight of our boys snuffed it while the captain was taking it easy
who knows where, somewhere safe and sound. What idiots we
were. The Krauts didn't even need to break a sweat to sink us.
Clearly they didn't need to lift a finger, because we were going
to scupper ourselves with no help from them.

That's the kind of thing we muttered to each other the night
we went on a bender in honour of the men who'd been sacri-
ficed by our cack-handed leaders. Then when our ship went
down we blathered on and on about the spies who must have
been laughing at how we'd been trounced by the Krauts on
one side and our own captains on the other.

I warned them, I can't keep my mouth shut. My pals used
to say: "Felix, you should keep quiet. You'll be accused of
inciting mutiny; the captain will do away with you." But I kept
on, I kept on . . . It'll take me a whole lifetime to get over my
anger at the captain and his officers who sent us to the mouth
of hell . . .

If by "negligence", you're thinking human error, like our
superiors were saying, claiming they were covering for us, you'd

have to be a bloody fool to believe that the second "accident" was just a coincidence. That's when things began to heat up.

In any case, it was time to take my leave from Guillaume's parents. It was essential that I kept a few things to myself.

But the only thing they'd really taken in from all I'd told them was that he'd swapped his shore leave with me that day, apparently quite arbitrarily.

And to be totally honest, they weren't the only ones to be surprised by that.

We had to find the perfect whipping boy – the spy, the one who'd been lying to us – so we could drag his name through the mud.

And a corpse, preferably . . . Easier that way. Job done.

Loubna, 2005

It was almost 6 a.m. Ali hadn't said a word for a while. He was sitting there enjoying the milky light so characteristic of daybreak in Casablanca, the pale city walls merging with the misty white sky. In the distance the voice of the muezzin calling the faithful to prayer suffused the dawn with a monotonous incantation. The darkness gradually dissipated, chased away by the sun, whose naked radiance draped the city in its silken embrace.

Ali hadn't moved. I wasn't sure if he was thinking about my cinema or his investments.

Quite suddenly, he decided it was time to go. Maybe he thought I was wasting his time and it was unthinkable for him to be sitting around not making any money.

"Can I give you a lift somewhere? Where do you live?"

"On Alger Street. Do you know it?"

He appeared to be a little thrown by my reply. Looking me up and down, he replied simply, "Great!"

He took off again at full speed. He must leave skid marks on the tarmac wherever he goes.

He knew exactly where to go. He didn't even need to ask me what number I lived at on the tiny street. He dropped me right in front of my building.

"It's here, right?"

"Yes, but how—?"

"Now I understand your taste for colonial buildings. It's not any old blood that you have flowing through your veins."

I had no idea what he was insinuating, or why, all of a sudden, there was an ironic smile playing on his lips.

"I grew up here. But I'm hardly the only person who did. What—?"

He looked at me with a mocking expression and interrupted me again.

"I don't know how you ended up in this building, but I imagine it belongs to your family. Am I right?"

I didn't like his tone. I hadn't slept all night and I wondered if he was looking for an excuse to bow out of the project. I stood on the pavement and slammed the car door shut.

What difference could it possibly make to him? I'd only known him a few hours. How rude he was, how ill-judged his comments. He lowered the passenger window and carried on addressing me.

"My grandfather was a diplomat. I know all the old stories of Casablanca. Your family was not what you would call respectable, that's all. But don't take it personally, Loubna. You're not responsible for what some of your family members got up to during the war."

He seemed pleased with the effect his words had on me, and I was pretty sure this wasn't going to work in my favour. He gave me a big grin before driving away. I didn't understand what he meant, and I didn't want to ask. Not him anyway.

My heart was beating wildly. The Maserati disappeared around the corner and I ran up the stairs.

I tried to piece together what I knew about my family, but with each step all I could dredge up were the scant bits of information I had. My mother hadn't kept it a secret, it was simply that my father hadn't known much and, according to her, had no desire to find out more: "He wanted to make his own history." Presumably the fact of being an orphan had motivated him from a young age to create a life rich in friendship and dreams, to make up for what he'd never had.

I've always lived in this building; my father too, as far as I know. My parents moved in when they got married. I have an apartment on the second floor. My mother is on the third floor.

My adoptive grandmother lived on the first floor with my grandfather, but they both died a long time ago.

Only my mother is still alive. It was still very early, but I convinced myself she must be up by now.

"Mama."

She was still in bed, sitting up and reading, propped up against some large cushions in her pink and blue dressing gown. She'd opened the window to enjoy the early-morning sunshine. She had another half an hour before she had to get up to get ready for work.

"Loubna! My goodness, look at you – did you just fall out of bed?"

"Mama, I've got a question. Who does this building belong to?"

She looked at me over the top of her glasses, an amused expression on her face.

"Loubna, you know perfectly well. Your grandmother."

"How could she afford to buy it if she worked at the hospital?"

Up until that moment I'd spent my entire life being fed these scraps of stories and accepting them unquestioningly. I'd shrugged off any rational or factual inconsistencies that might have destroyed the story I had created for myself. Some of my favourite films also had the most unlikely plots, and I had long ago decided that the story of my life was just like one of those.

"Not Zayna; your real grandmother! Your father's birth mother, the one who died in labour."

My mother got out of bed and closed the window. She came over and gave me a hug.

"Oh Loubna, surely you knew that?"

Gravity suddenly kicked in, and my body felt heavy. It had taken me thirty years to take an interest in all this. I knew so few concrete facts, and the little I did know I'd misunderstood. To the point that it turned out that a complete stranger, for whom "anything goes", knew that either my grandfather or my grandmother, or both of them, were "not what you would call respectable".

II

Time to Leave

Hélène, 1940

The thing that's really eating away at me isn't thinking about all that he was, but about all that he might have become.

His life was still just an outline, barely sketched out, and yet he had already lived so much. He was so full of life. He meant to marry Ginette when the war was over. They'd known each other since they were children. "Tell her she still has a special place in my heart," he always wrote in his letters home.

What a sweet, understated way to say: "I love her!" She adored him, was entirely faithful, completely unwavering about her choice. He was the one, and no one else. Her whole family loved my son. Her father worked on the railways; he drove the Amiens–Paris train until he lost the use of his hand in an accident. It was crushed between two pieces of white-hot metal. Every time he came home on leave it was Guillaume who did all the strenuous jobs around the house for them: painting the walls, fixing roof beams, replacing tiles, laying parquet, repairing a fence. He wasn't trying to earn Ginette's affection; he loved her so much anyway. They used to cycle across the poppy fields. What a waste, all those words of love drifting away on the summer breeze.

He had every reason to be happy. He was about to end his tour of duty in the navy and come home to start a family. Then the war broke out. He began to be sent further away, for longer periods, to places whose names we weren't allowed to know, on missions he couldn't talk about. Suddenly, we were all fearful. Now he only talked about the present, he no longer thought about the future.

He hadn't been home for over a year, and he no longer mentioned Ginette in his letters. Clearly war is incompatible with affection. It turns men into creatures who are incapable of loving or of being loved.

Liliane, 1940

My brother's absence is a terrible noise, an assault on the ears, an unimaginable brutality. For a week now, images have been circulating in my head: the sailor standing at the bottom of the front steps; my mother's strangled cry; my father running down the stairs; and springtime, which will never return.

It just didn't seem possible . . . Even though he'd enlisted in the navy and war had broken out, and he was obviously running a risk. We were all aware of it. It's like the bombing, the way every time you find yourself feeling a glimmer of optimism, it starts up again; every time you manage to convince yourself it's all going to be okay, that you've also got the right to be happy, and really, the person you love isn't actually right there where the war is happening, surely?

Right now, what matters is that the Germans don't make it over the Marne river like last time.

For several months now we've known things were beginning to heat up, even in North Africa. It was obvious from Guillaume's anxiety in his letters, all the things he'd stopped talking about. But he always said he'd been born under a lucky star: "I'm not going to die", "Death isn't interested in me", that sort of thing.

Until his last letters. He'd stopped thinking of death as a game of hide-and-seek or a game of poker. You could sense that he felt it all around him; he could smell it.

The day we got the news, I ran straight over to tell Ginette. She cried – of course, she was devastated – but her eyes were already red-rimmed. She'd just got back from staying with her cousin in Paris, and I had the feeling something had happened there, but she didn't want to talk about it. Family secrets, she told me.

We wept together for the man we had both lost.

Then Étienne turned up. He often goes to see her, since my brother stopped coming home on leave. He's always been crazy about her, but she was engaged to Guillaume.

Well, now the field is wide open! Perhaps he'll be tactful enough to wait a little before proposing himself as a replacement. After an hour I left the two of them alone. All I wanted was to shut myself in my bedroom, read Guillaume's letters, and dream about his return. I closed my eyes and began to fantasize about him coming back, turning up one day at the end of the war. We're sitting in the garden when he arrives without warning, sits down opposite us as if nothing's happened, a mischievous glint in his eyes. At first we can't believe it, for a few moments we're dumbstruck, then we jump on him, throw our arms around him, and never let him go.

These daydreams make me feel better, but they never last. They just allow me to escape the icy numbness that fills the house.

Life came to a complete standstill after Felix's visit. We were plunged into darkness, my parents and I. Everything, the sun, the springtime, it was all too painful.

We stayed at home, the shutters closed, keeping vigil over a body that would surely never be returned to us. This fact obsessed my father; he was desperate to see his son one last time. It was as though it was impossible for him to believe Guillaume's death was real without seeing his corpse. He was consumed by the idea that he wasn't really dead. But to hear my father say it, to hear these ideas emerge from the silence of his dreams, was like a sort of dark fairy tale, a madness, a curse.

I was simply an unwilling spectator of their grief, and it felt indecent.

Since we got the news, everything was in limbo, daily life just hanging in the air, suspended, like dust particles. My parents might as well have lost both their children that day. I think they would have behaved in exactly the same way.

Days went by. I stayed in my room with the curtains drawn, lying on the bed staring at the ceiling. I only left my refuge at night, plagued by hunger and thirst. The silence that reigned on the other side of my door was unbearable. You'd think we were all dead too.

Then something else began happening. Shouting, bursts of anger, rage. The first time, I was wrenched from my torpor by an awful shriek, followed by an uninterrupted torrent of abuse from my mother, who was screaming and ranting with fury. Grief turned into anger. She no longer did nothing but weep. She no longer wept at all. The silence that pervaded the house was broken and so too – and this was much worse – was the harmony that had always existed between my parents. She began attacking my father and repeating the same thing over and over: "You killed him! With your own hands, you realize that? This waste of life, it's all your fault. But you're going to pay for it, either God or I will make you pay for it. You'll pay, you'll see!"

I was stunned. I hid in the shadows, horrified at being party to this terrible revelation. When the screaming became completely unbearable, I turned on the wireless to cover the outbursts of hatred.

And all this time, while my family was unravelling, the German troops were advancing. We thought the war would be nipped in the bud by the end of 1939, but it promised to be rather more complicated. Germany had invaded Poland. The Somme region is not very far from the German border. Were we about to be invaded too? Since my brother, whom I had always believed to be immortal, had died, I'd lost all faith in the future. The fighting was getting closer every day. I was terrified at how my parents were frozen in their grief. My mother howled her hatred at my father, while he, floored by her accusations, stopped talking. I thought she was being horribly unjust. How could he be responsible for the death of his own son? It wasn't he who had caused the maintenance problem on the ship. It was just bad luck. My father had nothing to do with it. He had never even set foot in Morocco, and certainly not on board *La Railleuse*.

A week went by and I had to get out of the house. I wanted to see Ginette again. I'd left her all alone with her memories and I was feeling bad. But then again, she hadn't come to see me either.

And with good reason . . . It turned out she'd gone away. Her mother told me that the day after she heard the news, she'd packed her bags and gone back to her cousin's place in Paris. Her parents were worried. Not only for her but for all of us so near the border, all the shooting and the bloodshed. I didn't know what they were trying to tell me.

I have no idea if what they told me that day was the truth, but at the age of seventeen, and in the space of a few days, I came to understand that the real drama is played out in all the things that aren't said, in the words that one hesitates to say out loud for fear of wounding the other person, eventually deciding not to utter them at all.

I looked around the room. Something had changed. It looked like they were planning their departure, though they stopped short of saying they were, just as their daughter had.

"Are you absolutely sure she didn't leave a note for me?"

They didn't reply.

Her mother held out a copy of the previous day's *Paris-Soir*. It was dated Saturday, 11 May. The headlines were undeniably foreboding:

At dawn this morning Germany invaded Holland, Belgium and Luxembourg.

I could barely believe my eyes, and yet there it was:

Brussels under bombardment. Massive aerial assault on Amsterdam. The government in Luxembourg departs the capital. The Hague attacked by the Luftwaffe. Churchill replaces Chamberlain.

"What are you going to do? Are you leaving? Are you going to try and find her? Do you think we should all leave?"

They looked at me for a moment and then exchanged a glance. Her mother put her arms around me.

"Yes Lili, you should leave too, if you can . . ."

Ginette, 1940

The last time Guillaume came home on leave was in April, not long before war was declared. That was when he broke things off with me. It was as brief as it was brutal.

"Don't wait for me. I'm sorry."

I bombarded him with demands for an explanation. But he left, and I covered pages and pages with rage, threats and grief, tears that made the ink run all the way to the very edges of my sorrow.

Not only did I have to deal with the war, but I also had to endure his silence, and the abrupt end to his promise of love. Yet I carried on hoping. I hoped that I would persuade him to come back to me when he returned. I stopped writing to him, and kept my tears for night-time, when I lay alone. He didn't tell his family, not even his sister and best friend Lili.

Perhaps he was afraid he wouldn't come home. Perhaps he was leaving me precisely because he loved me so much. Once this thought had occurred to me, I couldn't shake it off. I would find out more when he was back. I resolved to wait patiently, more in love with him than ever. I decided that he must have resolved to shoulder the pain of our separation on his own.

Over a year went by with no news of him. I read and reread his letters, transforming their meagre emotion into proof of his desperate love for me. Despite what he had written, I was convinced that between the lines he was sending me a secret declaration. I began to hope again. He had promised we would spend our lives together – how could he drop me like that, for no reason? I was going mad. I had to know. If he didn't love me any more – which I didn't believe – he had to tell me, I had to see it in his eyes. They would not lie. At least then I would know. I decided to write him one last letter, filled with searing honesty.

You told me you loved me and I still believe you do, in spite of your last letter. I keep thinking back to the wonderful day we first met at the country fair in Péronne. Seven years ago. I fell in love with your face the minute I saw it, and I hoped with all my heart that one day it would be mine forever. I received a letter from a friend in Paris who told me that she knew a sailor from Toulon. I imagined it was you, that we might see each other again. That perhaps you return occasionally to French soil and we might meet. It is killing me not to see you any more. Every night I go to bed and weep. I kiss the photograph of the two of us, the one where we have our arms around each other, standing by our bicycles in the middle of the field of poppies. I still have the salty taste of your lips on mine.

I love you deeply and forever.

Eventually he wrote back. He was going to be on leave for a few days in Toulon, but it would be too brief to come all the way home to see his parents. He asked me to come so we could talk one last time, but made me swear not to say a word to his parents or his sister.

They don't need to know. Ginette, I'll say it again, even if I do owe you an explanation: all this is for your own good. Somebody else will make you happy as you deserve to be.

It didn't sound hopeful, and yet I clung to the thought of our reunion.

I pretended I was going to visit my cousin in Paris. My stomach was twisted up with nerves, but I was optimistic. We met up in Toulon at a hotel near the port.

Liliane, 1940

When I came home from seeing Ginette's parents, I was startled to see my father sitting in the garden in the shade of the great lime tree. That was where he had taught my brother and me to read, where we used to sit and bounce up and down on his knee, where he used to teach us things about life. This tree has been witness to all our secrets, troubles and joys. Since my brother died, I have often sat and talked with my father on this stone bench. Lately, he'd been trying to conceal his suffering; he'd slip his arm around my shoulders, but then his gaze would grow blank and, powerless to banish the horrors, I would get up and walk away.

Had my father really known what was going to happen? I suppose he might have deciphered it in the dust and the pollen that was lying among the tree roots, like a fortune teller with her tea leaves; he'd done everything he could to fight the devil who wanted his soul. The days that followed the news of my brother's death were the worst, even though all indications were that the war was only just beginning, and was going to cause us endless hours of terrible despair. In the week after our world was turned upside down, I would watch my father through my bedroom window, muttering incomprehensible words to the unbending, impassive lime tree.

"Papa? I'm going to see Ginette in Paris. I'll be back tomorrow, or at the latest the day after."

He lifted his face to me, seeming not to understand what I had just said. I hurried back to my room to pack a small suitcase. I had to go – to find Ginette and talk to her, but more importantly to keep myself from suffocating.

Carrying my suitcase, with a light coat draped over my shoulders, I tiptoed over to my mother's bed to tell her I was leaving. She was lying in the dark with her back to the door. She hadn't moved in hours, maybe days. She wasn't going to lift a finger to stop me. The war was approaching, and I was off.

Waiting at the station, lost in thought, I was distracted by a familiar voice. I looked up to see Felix standing there in front of me.

"I was just on my way over to see you," he said.

He had more things he wanted to tell me. Secrets to reveal. He said he'd rather take the train with me to Paris so that we could talk. He told me that for days he hadn't been able to think about anything but me – about both of us, my brother and me. He said there were things I needed to know, that he hadn't dared to tell my parents.

The more I looked at him, the more I realized what a state he was in. I tried to imagine what kind of friend he had been to Guillaume. I had no idea what they had been through together. But as Felix told me a few more personal, intimate things about my brother, it was as though he had conjured up Guillaume's presence. It was comforting and disturbing all at once.

Felix was in uniform. He was shorter than Guillaume and not as charismatic, but his light eyes and open smile made him appear immediately likeable. I hadn't paid a great deal of attention to him last time, this bearer of bad tidings. Now I could hear in the warmth of his voice how much he'd loved my brother. He put himself down when he spoke of Guillaume, as though he considered himself so much less impressive. Yet in the shyness he adopted as a way of covering up his natural way of speaking, which he seemed to think was too colloquial for me, there was something terribly touching. He liked me; I could see it in his eyes. He'd heard about me before he turned up at my parents' house. My brother had told him about me. I knew that, because we used to tell each other everything.

At one point, he got up and offered his seat to a pregnant woman. He stood, very straight, in his spotless white uniform, casting his eyes towards the ceiling while glancing at me occasionally out of the corner of his eye. We would have to continue our conversation later. For the first time since the beginning of the journey, I looked around and was aware of the effect his uniform was having on the people in the carriage. No one had eyes for anyone else, and I noticed the looks that the other women were giving him. It was as though they saw in him the hope of a ceasefire, or even an armistice.

Guillaume had taken to not wearing his uniform when he came home on leave. He'd been so proud of it the first few months, but gradually he had begun to regard it with something like horror.

People don't like the sight of us. They give us filthy looks in the street when we go out in the evening in Toulon, or wherever we are. They say that sailors are thieves, rapists, murderers. And they're not wrong.

My darling Liliane, never fall in love with a sailor. Time spent far from those you love goes too slowly to be lived honestly.

Last week we were in Casablanca, and we decided to visit the red-light district in Bousbir. Obviously we weren't drinking water. Sometimes you need a little something to help you forget you're a prisoner, that you actually volunteered to serve this sentence even though you're innocent of any crime. I wanted to travel the world, but all I've seen is the brutality of human nature.

Anyway, I was with some friends who've got a thing for the women who display their charms there.

Marcel from Marseille had been stringing along this lady friend of his for days, swearing his love for her. It was all part of a plan to send her off to Marseille to go on the game in one of the shady parts of town. He promised her she'd be completely safe there – she'd be dealing with men who were much more civilized than sailors whose appetites were sharp-ened after days and weeks of solitude at sea. And when he returned home he'd marry her. I bet you a thousand francs he's her pimp now, and madly proud of his little scheme: "Everyone puts his money where it works for them, Guillaume!" Well, I was a bit the worse for wear and before I could stop myself, I planted my fist in his face. They banged me up in solitary for three days because of him, but I swear to God I'm not a bit sorry.

We stand out in every place we stop. We're the people who spend the most in the red-light district, in Marseille, Algiers, Casablanca. In Casablanca they've even set up a special bus line to take us there. But don't worry, tourists love to go there too. They call it "local colour".

I was in such a hurry to see the world, and how disap-pointing are my fellow inhabitants. My sailor mates, French, English or American, all they want is to get an eyeful of the naked women in Bousbir and the slums on the other side in Ben M'Sik. They're barely women. More like young girls your age, little sister. Most of them are barely sixteen and already their lives are committed to the medina of earthly pleasures. The moneyed colonials prefer its blinding white walls, warmed by the sun, to the prosperous squares and avenues that line the port of Casablanca. That's where they take their afternoon constitutionals, or they strut along the Avenue de la Gare, bordered by palm trees, or linger on café terraces on the Square of France, or even in the alleyways of the medina or Lyautey Park. And then when night falls, they venture down the winding alleyways of the red-light district, as though they're going on an adventure, or a safari. It's a kind of underworld in the heart of the wealthy dis-trict, with its sprawling cafés, its packed restaurants and theatres. Everything encourages consumption, whether under-neath the arches along the Boulevard de la Gare or in the strange otherworld of the forbidden city: the heady frag-rance of olives and argan oil, the fresh smell of saffron and

*mandarins, the velvety aroma of cinnamon and orange flower
water on pastry stalls, or on a flash of dark skin. It's a feast
for the senses; for the soul, it's something else.*

*I still have 876 days left of 1,890. I'm counting down the
days, my beloved Lili.*

My brother told me everything. We shared our deepest
secrets with each other; there was no barrier between us at
all. He knew things I'd never have been able to tell any of my
friends so honestly and with such a lack of restraint. Now he
has taken these secrets to the grave, along with his own.

I was lost in thought. Felix gently touched my shoulder to
let me know we'd arrived in Paris. The station was terribly
crowded; I wasn't used to such a hectic, bustling atmosphere.
Felix took down my suitcase from the luggage rack and refused
to give it to me.

"I have a little bit of time. I'll walk with you to your friend's
house before I catch the train for Toulon."

My neighbour stood up wearily, holding his huge belly with
one hand and a duffel bag with the other. He gave me a dark
look. I was relieved Felix was coming with me; it felt like my
brother was still here, keeping an eye on me. I told him where
Eugénie lived. She was the cousin Ginette was staying with.

"It's not far, it won't take long to get there."

We left the station and were immediately assailed by newspaper sellers yelling out at the top of their voices headlines
from *Progrès*, *Paris-Soir* and the *Petit Journal*:

France Under Attack

Pushback in the Northeast by the German Army

Intense German Pressure in Flanders

I'd already been to the city to stay with Eugénie for the
occasional weekend, thrilling to the heady delights of Parisian

life, but now as we walked through the streets other pedestrians reacted to our slower pace with an intense irritability quite unlike what I was used to. An atmosphere of free and easy pleasure had given way to strained expressions and a nervous pace.

There was something in the air, even though people were still refusing to believe that their daily lives were about to be turned upside down.

Felix walked along in silence, staring at the Parisians, who stared back disdainfully, sometimes addressing him with overt hostility:

"What are you doing here? Why aren't you at the front, fighting like a real man, instead of lazing around here with your pretty little lady friend . . ."

"Hey, mate, if we're meant to be counting on blokes like you, it'll be no surprise if the Krauts make it here easy as a hot knife through butter!"

Several times I grabbed his arm to keep him from throwing a punch at someone. There was no need to add any more reckless damage to the situation.

Even though the Germans were getting closer, more than a few people still seemed confident:

"Don't you worry! We've got the Maginot Line. We learned our lesson last time. We're not going to give those Krauts an inch. They'll break their teeth trying to get through, you'll see!"

Even for the least optimistic observer, there was frank disbelief at the idea that Paris could ever be taken. It couldn't possibly fall into German hands, that was simply out of the question.

In a café near the station I paid for a telephone call to let my parents know I'd arrived. No one answered. I'd have to try again the next day. We continued in the direction of Eugénie's apartment. I'd left Ginette alone with her sadness, and then she had taken off without telling me. I had the feeling that something strange had happened while my back was turned.

We reached Eugénie's neighbourhood. As we turned a corner we caught the sun in our eyes, and for the first time I noticed the beautiful weather, how lovely and clear the sky was. I felt a brief moment of joy, distracting me from the disturbing sight before me.

Most of the shops were shuttered. Almost all were plastered with posters and signs forbidding entry. Whole families were on the move. People were hurrying, dragging suitcases along the pavement. A strange silence had fallen on the growing crowd. A few straggling customers were finishing their coffees on a café terrace, lost in their newspapers, grave expressions on their faces. I bought a newspaper from a man who was in such a hurry he hadn't even locked up his kiosk.

"I don't have time. I have to go. Take it, miss – it's a gift."

Leaning into each other as we walked down Faubourg-Saint-Denis Street, we scanned the headlines. We turned onto Paradis Street. Passers-by knocked into us, but I barely noticed. I was horrified. The situation seemed to be worsening by the hour.

Night was falling and Felix took my hand. We were never going to get there. The crowd was growing denser, and as we made our way towards the north of the city we found ourselves walking against a great tide of people going in the other direction. In front of the door of the building where Eugénie lived in a tiny maid's room up in the attic, a couple stood, wrapped in a tight embrace. He was in uniform, and she was carrying a suitcase. They were bidding each other farewell, weeping. I couldn't help staring at them, totally unaware of the time passing, while Felix shielded me from the flood of panicking people. I thought of Ginette and my brother. I thought of all the couples all over this wretched country, forced to say goodbye to each other, weeping, leaving behind them the people they loved the most.

"Lili? What are you doing here?"

The familiar voice of Eugénie brought me to my senses.

"I came to see Ginette. Her parents told me she was with you."

She stared at me. She looked confused.

"But don't you know?"

My surprised expression made it clear that I didn't.

"She's not here. She's gone away, with him. I'm off too," she said, pointing to her luggage.

"What do you mean? He's dead."

"I promise you he is as alive and kicking as anyone could ever hope to be."

My heart began to thump so hard that I felt my chest swelling. My legs began to shake. On the brink of unconsciousness, I heard myself cry out, "Where did they go?"

A man walked into me. I let go of Felix's hand, hurrying ahead to catch up with Eugénie. She answered me without turning round:

"To her family in the south, I think."

I almost collapsed. Tears were rolling down my cheeks. My brother wasn't dead after all. Eugénie, clearly in a great hurry, was running now, and I couldn't keep up with her.

A car drew up alongside us and stopped.

"They're entitled to a bit of happiness," she said, as she climbed into the gleaming black Ford.

"Hurry, Eugénie, get in! What about your friend there?"

The news was so extraordinary, my joy so great, my emotions so overwhelming. I called out to Felix. My legs were unsteady. I'd lost sight of him, caught up in the crowd. I shouted out his name again, but my voice was lost in the din. My legs couldn't hold me any more; the shock of hope suddenly snatched away all my strength. Waves of unfamiliar, worried faces passed in front of my eyes, turning into trails of colour and light. No one even glanced at me. I was invisible. The world began to spin. My vision grew blurred and all I can remember is a stream of stars.

It happened in a flash. I must have fainted and taken a moment or two to come round. Felix was holding me in his arms and looking at me with an anxious expression on his face. His hand, trembling very slightly, was gently stroking my cheek. I sat up with a jerk. The car, with Eugénie in it, had driven off.

I raised my eyes to the ongoing ballet of passers-by overtaking and knocking into one another as they hurried past. The sense of panic was growing. There was no time to lose. Felix helped me to my feet.

I wasn't walking, I was floating. Felix pulled me along behind him while I remained lost in my thoughts. My brother had eloped with Ginette. He was alive . . . My beloved brother was going to be part of my life after all. He might be an enemy of our country, but he was alive, breathing the same air as I, warming himself in the same sunlight. He must have come up with his plan to run away with her several days ago, if not weeks. I was ridiculously excited about this turn of events. Of course neither of them could have said a word about it to anyone; they had to be sure to put as few people as possible in danger. My brother didn't want to make the rest of us traitors.

Felix had told me that Guillaume had changed over recent weeks, that he'd begun to seem like a different person. He had started talking about the futility of war, the way it sapped the morale of his comrades. He must already have been plotting his escape.

From that moment on, I was obsessed with one thing and one thing only: to find out where they were. I absolutely had to.

Loubna, 2005

I had to find some trace of them. I had to find some trace of my grandparents to understand what Ali was alluding to. His words echoed constantly in my mind: "Your family was not what you would call respectable."

I paced up and down my apartment like a caged animal. I lay down and tried to sleep but, however hard I tried, my eyes remained wide open, staring at the ceiling as if somehow it might hold the key to understanding everything.

I didn't tell my mother what Ali had said about our family. I didn't want her to know that was how people thought of us.

By now it was nine o'clock in the morning and I had been pondering all this for nearly three hours. Anis, my best friend, would be at the mosque by now. I put on my denim jacket and went out without eating or showering. I didn't even brush my hair.

The Hassan II mosque, the symbol of Casablanca, had stood proudly facing the crashing waves on the seafront since 1993, the year I turned fifteen. I remember how impatient we were to find out what the gigantic edifice was going to look like. Now Anis works part time there as a guide. He teaches history in a few different schools and supplements his income with odd jobs that he gets through friends: guided tours of the Hassan II mosque, private tutoring, and night shifts in libraries and archives.

I slipped inside. All the attendants and security guards there know me, and they greeted me with a little wave. I often pop by to see Anis, and they let me in, as long as I'm discreet.

Sometimes I wait for him to finish work and then we go and eat doughnuts and watch the kids jump the waves.

I wanted to surprise him, so I tiptoed barefoot over the carpets that covered the marble floor of the immense prayer space where tourists are allowed in during fixed opening hours. I made my way over to his group at the precise moment that he was telling his favourite joke about the roof that slides open in warm weather: "You're standing in the only open-top mosque in the world."

The group of tourists, a little surprised, burst out laughing. Before anyone could say anything, I broke in: "What speed can it get up to on the motorway?"

He pretended to frown, but I saw him wink. I gestured to him that I would wait for him outside and tiptoed away.

Outside, the blinding sun reflected off the old city walls, glistening with dust and salt. I leaned against a ledge and looked out to sea. Off to the right was the port and its fishing trawlers.

A quarter of an hour later Anis joined me on the ramparts. He was tall and rangy, and there was a kind of feline elegance about him as he approached. He hadn't shaved for a few days, and it suited him. It flattered his features and highlighted his lovely, almond-shaped eyes. He must have had a girlfriend or two who'd encouraged him to let his beard grow a bit.

I told him about the previous night with Ali. I noticed him frown at the mention of his name. I repeated word for word what Ali had said and then told him the real reason for my visit.

"Anis, I've never asked you to do anything for me, have I?"

His expression had tightened while I was telling him about Ali. Now he snorted with laughter.

"I'll tell that to my father – he'll be very amused."

"But you and Osman love me, you weren't doing me favours. I said I never *asked* you for anything – do you see the difference? But now I have to know. I know you always said I should find out more about my family, and I never listened to you."

He put a finger on my lips and gestured to me to stop talking. Then he closed his eyes and tilted his face towards the sun. Solemnly, he declared:

"Loubna, this is the first time in my entire life that you've told me I'm right. Let me enjoy it for a few minutes."

I poked him gently in the ribs and he burst out laughing, before adding, suddenly serious:

"History is complicated, and the history of that period especially so . . . It was wartime, obviously. Just like History with a capital H, personal history is like a river – you have to go back to its source to understand it. I've been doing research on your behalf for years! I knew you'd want to know one day."

I stared at him, astonished. I'd had no idea. He went on:

"A few years ago, you mentioned the name of your grandfather. I didn't know who he was. At the time I had no information about him at all, but I had a feeling his surname was German. Guillaume Straub, is that right?"

Astonishingly, the thought had never occurred to me. As far as I'd been aware, he was French. Morocco had always been in the Free Zone; I couldn't imagine what a German would have been doing in Casablanca. As Anis continued talking, the nightmare scenario that I was the granddaughter of a Nazi began scrolling through my mind. I wondered if I hadn't been right after all to have always refused to stir up old memories.

"At the time there were a lot of Europeans living in Casablanca: French, British and German. A few things made me wonder if he might be German. Straub – it certainly sounds German. And Guillaume is the French name of the last Kaiser, Wilhelm II, who died in 1941."

I don't even know my grandmother's name. She died before she could tell the woman who adopted my father what she was called. She just managed to gasp the name of the baby's father as she lay dying.

I felt a jolt of disgust. A German, in 1940 . . . Enlisted right at the very beginning of the war. A Nazi . . . I didn't want to delve any further into the past if it meant I was going to find out that my grandfather was an admirer of Hitler. Ali's words started to take on new meaning: "Your family was not what you would call respectable." Was that why? What about my grandmother? Who was she? Was she German too? Or a Frenchwoman abandoned by her man at the very beginning of the war? Or a Moroccan woman who'd been seduced – or, worse, raped – by a Nazi?

Perhaps that was why my father became a political militant. He must have had all these questions going round and round in his head, have been frustrated not to have any answers. Or maybe, like me today, he preferred not to know; maybe he was too afraid that the truth would be unbearable. It was appalling enough that his father had abandoned the woman who was carrying his child. What kind of man behaves like that? And what was she doing in a military hospital?

In an instant, my whole life, all my fantasies, were collapsing. Anis interrupted my self-destructive musings.

"Anyway, it turned out that he was actually French after all. Eventually I found out some stuff about him. But I lost a lot of time following this false lead."

He hesitated.

"That said, what I discovered doesn't tell us anything about his political beliefs, or what he got up to during the war . . . And he had the perfect name for someone who wanted to make trouble or change sides . . ."

Anis hoisted his bag over his shoulder and looked ready to go. Tactfully, he brought our conversation to an end. He was, as ever, being extremely considerate about this. Now I knew what my best friend had been up to, working silently on my behalf, ready to surprise me the day I was ready to find out, if that time ever came. I was very touched.

"I'll bring all the stuff I've got at home over this evening. I know who to talk to if you want to find out more. As long as you don't have all the details – and perhaps you never will – you'll only know the tip of the iceberg. What that bastard Ali told you, in other words. You might be afraid of what you'll find out, but you have to tell yourself that this is part of what's made you who you are. You'll finally have some answers to the questions you've been asking yourself forever, without even knowing."

Felix, 1940

Hearing the news was like having a building come crashing down on top of us. He wasn't dead. What a shock. My knees buckled. Lili fainted, but luckily I caught her just in time.

A single thought was occupying my head: it's not like there are a thousand ways to disappear off the face of the earth. You didn't have to be a genius to realize that it was quite some coincidence, him disappearing and then the explosion. It was bloody convenient for Guillaume, put it that way . . .

Good God . . . I can't believe he blew up the ship just so he could run away with some bird. It's just not possible.

I took Lili's hand in mine and held on tight. I didn't want to lose her again in the crowd. Thoughts kept popping into my mind, like boxes piling up one on top of the other. Obviously I wasn't going to say anything to her – she was his sister, after all – before I was sure.

We were still holding hands as we made our way to the station. I didn't want her to go back north: I knew there'd be roadblocks. I hadn't known her long, but I was pretty sure I wanted to get to know her better.

We didn't talk. As we walked, we were each trying to make sense of what we'd just learned . . . I kept drifting off into my thoughts, then forcing myself back into the present to check how she was doing. She didn't look like things were much clearer for her; her eyes were fixed on her feet, and she certainly wasn't going to find any answers there.

Trying to keep a cool head, I kept saying to myself: "Felix, think hard: what exactly happened on the day of the explosion, after you got back?"

I played it all over repeatedly in my head, like a film on a loop. I remembered racing off so I could make the most of my forty-eight hours of freedom, thinking I'd grill Guillaume later to find out why he'd let me take his place. It was awfully charitable of him, but I wasn't such a fool that it didn't occur to me that there must have been something in it for him.

The first step I took onto dry land I saw her, standing there as usual, and I turned back towards him, ready to give him a cheeky wink. I'd already planned my jibe for when I saw him two days later: "Eh, Guillaume! Your lady friend was waiting for you in the port. She must have been a bit disappointed when it wasn't you she saw coming down the gangplank!"

I remember he didn't look me in the eye, but I noticed him giving her a dark look. At the time I suppose I thought she must be one of those clingy types, and that he'd grown sick of her. It's true she was always hanging around . . . He muttered something, but I couldn't hear what.

I wasn't even halfway through my leave when news of the tragedy was all over Casablanca. Weeping and wailing everywhere. People shouting themselves hoarse, everyone yelling: "It blew up . . . bodies everywhere . . ." No one could get any more information. But I didn't need it spelled out. A ship was on fire. It had all kicked off again. I ran as fast as I could; when I reached a metal railing, I clambered up it to get a view of the port and the pandemonium. Straight away I saw it was my ship.

What a sight . . . A window onto my worst nightmare . . . People dragging bodies out of the water, the living, the dead, body parts everywhere. It was complete chaos. I remember doubling over and vomiting from the shock of it.

Some of the lads had been sent to the military hospital at Ben M'sik. There were hardly any survivors. Almost everyone died of their wounds. All off to the great cemetery in the sky. They fell like flies.

Marcel from Marseille, he made it out. When he was able to talk, all he could really describe was impressions . . . He hadn't had time to see a thing. An explosion. Noise, a hellish din. He was thrown into the air. He remembered flying, falling . . . it did't hurt because he'd already passed out. When he came to, he was in the military hospital. That was it. Details would come back to him later.

My own head's stuffed full of details. Things I'd rather not remember. We spent the whole day, mates and Moroccans who rushed to help us, separating the men who were to be dispatched to hospital and those bound for the morgue. There weren't many men on board *La Railleuse*. Nothing like the gigantic *Pluton*. Two hundred died on the *Pluton*. After a while they gave up trying to find all the body parts.

There were only twenty-eight on board *La Railleuse* the day it blew up. Some were on leave, or off duty, and they rushed back – along with the captain, who'd had the brilliant idea of going for a walk around the port to clear his head. We stood there like idiots, going over what had happened again and again. We kept asking him, "What do we do now, Captain?"

I suddenly felt a wave of dizziness come over me as I realized something – I never saw Guillaume's body. And I was one of the people counting the bodies. In all the chaos, I didn't even think it was strange. I suppose we thought he'd been sucked into the sea and he'd be spat out a few weeks later, so none of us made a big deal of it. But a corpse that disappears, that's not exactly a trivial detail, if you think about it.

Especially since – well how about that – it's my mate Guillaume who's missing, and now I discover he's pulled off a disappearing act.

Two days after the explosion, the captain gave me a few days' leave. I didn't have a ship any more, or a posting, but he sent me on a mission to visit the families of some of the mates I knew well.

I absolutely have to find a way to get back to Casablanca . . . Some of the lads must have seen or known something. And there was that girl standing on the quay exchanging looks with him. She'd been there almost every day in the period leading up to the explosion, wrapped in a djellaba like she didn't want to be recognized.

Lili and I boarded the train. But all through the journey I couldn't shake the feeling that there were too many peculiarities about this whole story for things to be explained away as pure coincidence. And the girl at the port, that seemed more of a serious matter now. It remained to be seen whether all of this would end up keeping me awake at night . . .

Liliane, 1940

I was lost in thought, utterly stunned by the news. I kept turning it over in my mind: my brother the deserter; I couldn't stop thinking what an amazing revelation it was. This meant he wasn't dead – he was safe somewhere.

And just like that, I was filled with hope again. All that mattered was my brother was alive. I much preferred a spy who was alive to an obedient sailor who was dead. Our father had taught us German because he'd grown up with the language, and it had come in useful during the First World War. Because he knew the language, he'd been able to understand the orders that the German generals gave their soldiers, and he'd avoided a few beatings. It had saved his skin. So now I decided that history had repeated itself, and I didn't care if it had led to betrayal.

I remembered the way my mother had kept shouting: "It's all your fault!" Maybe that was what she blamed him for, that he'd brought us up as secret Germans. Because we weren't supposed to tell anyone that we knew the language. He'd even taught us to pretend not to understand it. Our father felt pulled in two directions. During the war he'd been forced to make a choice; he'd made it and he'd stuck to it; but he always used to tell us that the men on the other side "were exactly the same as us. They didn't deserve to die any more than we did." These were the ideas we'd grown up with. Our father believed that war was an aberration. He came back from the trenches a fervent pacifist, and when Guillaume announced he wanted to join the navy it came as a terrible shock.

So what if he'd gone over to the Germans, was a traitor and

a deserter? He was still my brother. I couldn't wait to tell my parents. They would certainly react like I had. I decided to send them a telegram, as enigmatic as possible. We'd been at war for months and I was sure the censors were going through every communication with a fine-tooth comb, looking for anything suspicious.

Father, Mother. Am in Paris. Guillaume still not found. Will explain.

Felix tried to hush my questioning and my second guessing. He was in a hurry to get to Austerlitz railway station. Right now, other things were more important. The atmosphere was making us extremely tense, and he was trying to persuade me not to go home to the north.

"You have to come with me. Don't make the mistake of going home to your parents. You'll see them again when things calm down."

On the way to Paris we'd seen trains filled with soldiers heading east towards enemy lines, hoping to attack the border and crush the enemy with a rain of gunfire. All young men had been mobilized as a matter of urgency to join the forces fighting on the eastern front. Felix was right, it made no sense to head back there. It was too late. The days we'd spent as if at an extended wake had distanced us from the world, which seemed to be changing by the minute.

Since I had nowhere to go, Felix bought me a ticket for the train he was taking to Toulouse. He wanted to go and see his sister and to entrust me to her before he went back to Toulon. He kept saying I had to think about finding a safe place to stay, and I could worry about everything else later. For the time being I could stay with his sister, which would give me time to think.

We stood waiting on the platform. I hadn't stopped clutching his hand for what seemed like hours. I'd long ago stopped counting the minutes.

An accordionist began, falteringly, to play the first notes of a tune by Fréhel. A woman, her voice quavering from trying not to weep, began to sing. I could hear the tears in her voice as it grew stronger against the din that echoed around the glass-roofed station. In a matter of moments, the crowd fell silent, as everyone listened to the woman's heart-breaking lament. She was singing for her lover, who had just boarded the train.

> *Where have all my lovers gone?*
> *Bound to my sadness, at night,*
> *Nothing to hold me, I am all alone,*
> *My heart, like flotsam,*
> *Tossed around on the waves.*
> *How happy I once was,*
> *So many admirers,*
> *Parties galore.*
> *Now I am bound to my suffering,*
> *Enslaved to my memories.*

Around her, a few last silent, tearful farewell embraces and whispered prayers were taking place on the platform. Hers was the only voice that could be heard. The other travellers held their breath as if trying to forget they were there.

> *Where have all my lovers gone*
> *Who loved me once, when I was beautiful?*

Too soon, the train began to move.

> *Then the night is over,*
> *And when daybreak comes,*
> *The dawn weeps with me.*

The song faded away with the dusk, and the train, its side bristling with the arms of soldiers waving one last time, disappeared over the horizon.

Those I loved, who
Loved me by night
Now they fade away
In the pale morning light.
My eyes grow misty.
It's as if I were still
Holding them in my arms,
Like puppets on a string.

The train was packed, even more so than the one we'd arrived on in the morning. All the seats were occupied. We stood in the corridor pressed up against each other, surrounded by suitcases and baskets. Newborn babies cried and adults remained hushed. We stood for hours, and each time we drew into a station there was a great wave of agitation – cries of despair, people rushing to grab a place in one of the carriages. We found ourselves more and more squeezed up against each other. At Orléans I had to pull my head back so as not to bump into Felix as we talked. By the time we reached Châteauroux he only had to whisper in my ear, and I could feel his breath on my neck. By Limoges, our chests were almost touching.

Through the windows we watched long columns of people and carts heading south. Silhouettes of people bent double, as if leaning towards inevitable suffering. There we were, right in the middle of the chaos, and yet it felt like we were all alone in the world. When he laid the lightest of kisses on my lips, it felt like the war was over.

Hélène, 1940

In the blink of an eye, the war took on an air of defeat. The shooting, the bombing, the sirens heralding Stukas swooping down to release a salvo of deadly bombs. My whole being recognized the fear, like an old acquaintance spotted disappearing around the corner, quite unchanged. You thought they were dead, and then there they were, lurking in the shadows, on the lookout for someone to feed them. I'd been gripped by dread for so long during the last war that when it returned it instinctively fitted like a glove. We'd had only the briefest time to catch our breath and recover our dreams. My previous life, my children – it had all been just a fantasy, in the end.

War had only just begun and yet already it was getting close. But Lucien and I wanted to wait for Lili.

The closer the gunfire got, the more it seemed we were bound for defeat. If we stayed, it wouldn't be long before it was too late to leave. It was our second loss in a matter of days. Our son had already been taken from us. Were we really going to have to flee our home without our daughter, too? People were saying that the Germans were already at the Somme river, already at the ports of the Pas-de-Calais. We had to get out. The air attacks were getting closer by the hour. Our army was no match for the Germans – the Wehrmacht was moving forward as though through already conquered territory. How easy they made it look, and lightning fast. They were proceeding methodically: a day of offensive advance, a day of calm, and so on, again and again. They were disciplined, precise and terribly efficient. Not only had we been defeated at every stage, but they were already imposing their rhythm, their rules. Our troops were trying, somewhat clumsily, to carry out makeshift repairs to tanks and trucks, but it was almost impossible to find petrol to fill the armoured vehicles. A few minor victories were not enough to make up for the enemy's advances as they trampled all our old assumptions. We'd always believed the River Meuse was daunting, unbreachable. Wrong.

We were on the point of becoming German. We'd be crushed. Occupied. The noise was growing; the desperate cries of people rushing south by foot.

We had just heard on the radio that the bridges over the Meuse had not been destroyed in time and the panzer divisions were speeding towards us, meeting no resistance. They were heading straight for Arras and Amiens.

I'd seen it all before in 1914. I knew what was going to happen. Wehrmacht officers would kill all those who were unlucky enough to cross their path, seize their homes and move in, giving the owners absolutely no say in the matter. We had no choice but to leave everything behind. In the space of barely an hour, we gathered up what seemed essential: some clothes, Guillaume's letters . . . and abandoned all the other bits and pieces that make up a life.

Memories of the last war came flooding back. I wouldn't admit it to anyone, but we had fun. Ah yes, what fun we had! We women had to join the war effort, and so in 1915 I started working in a munitions factory in Amiens. It was terribly hard work. You had to hold a seven-kilo shell in one hand to adjust the cover plate, close it again and put it down on the other side, and then on to the next. It felt like saving the life of a child, snatching them back from their fate in the trenches. I lifted tens of thousands each day, in twelve-hour shifts. In the newspapers they said if we were arrested, the Allies would lose the war in twenty minutes. Our men needed us, and we felt useful. The whole country was counting on us, and it was a marvellous feeling. We were expected to do more than domestic tasks. For the first time we were earning our own money. The war gave us what we had never dared hope for.

With the other girls from the factory we organized our daily lives in a most enjoyable way, in spite of the exhaustion, and nothing came between us and the mutual support and friendship that made us feel alive. The only thing that broke our happy tension was the letters that contained bad news. We lived in a sort of dormitory and didn't mind the lack of privacy; quite the opposite, in fact – our shared life was all about conviviality and solidarity. We even had a well-earned glass of red wine every day at lunchtime. Of course we missed our men, but – it's terrible to admit, and I would never say it out loud – I've never laughed so much and, though the work was hard, it gave us all a reason for being. None of us would have denied how much we loved it.

At the end of the war, we were earning almost as much as the men for the same work. For some of us, myself included, the aftermath of the war was terrible, partly for that reason. From one day to the next we were back to being housewives. Our men, those who were in good health, were in a hurry to get back to work, to recover their former lives. They wanted to spoil us, so that – and they wouldn't admit this out loud either, I'm sure – they could take back the status that we had usurped.

During the war there was Gaston, the foreman, who managed to hold on to his cushy job right to the end, strutting around in his role as the only cockerel left in the farmyard. He was always chasing our skirts while our men were at the front. I was his favourite . . . and I admit I encouraged him. And even though I did nothing to be ashamed of, I still wouldn't want Lucien to know that I was that kind of girl. There are good and bad aspects to war. It makes you confront your most heartfelt emotions. It's the fear in your belly that you know better than anything. And it's in extreme situations that you feel the most alive. After the last war ended, I cried every night into my pillow at having to unlearn freedom. I knew I didn't have the strength to go through that again.

When I was almost at the car I slowed down, barely aware of what I was doing. Every minute counted, but I wanted to wait for my daughter. The neighbouring village had been bombed. Lucien lowered his eyes. Our village would be the next to surrender. We were going to lose our second child. The stomach-churning fear was indescribable. It burrowed into us, devoured us.

The whole country was going through hell again. I was weeping with rage as Lucien and I drove through the roads of Amiens, overtaking the endless column of desolate souls walking south. The aerial attacks were getting closer and we knew that most of these people would never be seen again. Their drawn, anxious faces; their lives reduced to one hand held out to a child struggling to keep up, a small suitcase in the other, feet dragging over the cobbles. So little was left, the greater part of our lives already behind us.

We were leaving a part of the world that was no longer ours. The danger was imminent, and we had no idea if we'd left in time. Maybe it was already too late. Behind us, in the distance, bombs were already falling on Amiens.

Instinctively, Lucien knew to avoid the main roads, which were sure to be the next strategic target. All the old reflexes of wartime came back to him, and that was what saved our lives. He took frequent detours, to avoid being slowed down by the columns of "deserters", as Marshal Pétain called the people fleeing. They were ideal targets for air strikes. We drove for miles and miles, taking small roads heading west. And the bombs didn't take long to arrive. From a distance we saw the diving Stukas, heard them roar as they dropped their bombs on civilian targets. Now people can no longer say that doesn't happen.

I couldn't stop thinking about Lili. I wept with frustration that we hadn't waited for her. Lucien and I had lost everything. Our children, our home. I prayed for a bomb to fall on us, for Lucien to take the wrong road, for the planes from hell to head west and target us.

For it all to be over! I couldn't bear to go through what awaited us.

Lucien, 1940

We drove in silence away from the long line of people fleeing the aerial bombardments. After days of anxious travelling, we eventually made it to Clermont-Ferrand, where we had family. We had no news of Lili, and Hélène and I hadn't exchanged a single word since we'd left. Her refusal to speak made the silence of our son's absence weigh even more heavily on me. A terrible, endless silence that would never again be broken by a burst of laughter.

When he saw us drive into the courtyard, François, Hélène's cousin, dropped his newspaper and ran to greet us.

"I'm so happy to see you! I thought you'd all been killed."

He clasped me in a tight embrace, but his joy was punctured by Hélène's terse response and her exhausted face, consumed by sorrow.

"It should have been us." Our children weren't with us. He realized what she was saying and threw a look at his wife who stood a few feet away. We embraced in silence.

"We had no idea where to go. Up north it's—"

"A disaster! Yes, we heard."

He picked up the newspaper.

"Have you seen this? We are still fighting, magnificently. *Mag-ni-fi-cent-ly!* If it was so magnificent, you wouldn't be here, let's face it . . ."

He too was a veteran of the Great War.

"You know exactly how it goes, François . . . The roads, the bridges, all crowded with fleeing civilians. French, Belgian, Luxembourgeois. All heading south, of course. We only just avoided being machine-gunned by the Italians . . . And we came by car. Think of all those poor people walking for days. At least it's not cold. It's lucky it's June."

François obviously didn't want to talk about it with Hélène looking so despondent – I could see her expression made him uncomfortable. I hardly recognized her. Yes, we were exhausted, it had been a long and difficult journey, several times we thought we were going to die, but this was different.

As a way of ending the conversation, François declared: "We aren't going to let ourselves be beaten. We have Marshal Pétain. He saved us once, and he'll save us again."

I was not so sure. The spirit of revenge had been growing in Germany since the humiliating defeat of 1918. I had distant cousins in the Ruhr with whom I maintained a sporadic correspondence, in spite of the war and the passing of time. Throughout the 1920s, we'd all acknowledged that on both sides we had been duped by our leaders, we were all victims of the war, and there was no point in our quarrelling. But lately the tone had begun to change.

The treaty of Versailles had forced my cousins to their knees. A great many innocent people had paid the price for a few guilty ones, for the wartime destruction that they hadn't wanted any more than we had.

In July 1932, Ilse, my first cousin Helmut's daughter, came to stay with us. She was the same age as Lili and was very impressed by Paris, constantly comparing its splendours to the misery that prevailed in Berlin and the rest of the country. I remember one Sunday we went to buy chocolate to make a mocha cake. Ilse was wide-eyed at what seemed to her quite unseemly extravagance. Born after the war, she had only eaten a few pieces of chocolate in her entire life, and then only at Christmas. We melted it and beat it with butter and egg yolks to prepare the ganache to be spread between two slices of moist sponge cake, generously sprinkled with sugar syrup and a little cognac.

Incredulous, Ilse watched the cake being made, shocked to see so much butter and chocolate melted, mixed and beaten.

Taking tiny bites, she began to cry. When she recovered herself, she only stopped eating to say, "France is the richest country in the world!" before gobbling up her slice in a few huge spoonfuls.

Helmut wrote to me afterwards, warmly thanking me for having had Ilse to stay, and gently teasing me for the notions of luxury that I had put into her head. Lili, who was a little taller than her, gave Ilse two of her dresses, and Hélène made her two blouses in fine silk.

"She struts around the village, and all she can talk about is mocha cake and French wine! I too am rather nostalgic for Hélène's baking, as I am sure you can imagine. We have to save our butter for special occasions. And once a year we melt a square of chocolate under our tongues."

In a few years, the inflation and crisis of the 1930s had given way to economic recovery after Hitler came to power, and the talk had changed.

"It's our turn to reap the benefits now! At last I can boast about having as nice a car as you. Our currency is stronger and finally we can have some fun. I might even buy a car for Ilse. I bet you're wondering how I'm going to manage that. On credit! I can't say I like Hitler's style, but I have to admit he's got us out of our misery, when we thought it was going to go on forever. You can't imagine what it was like for us – you were on the right side at the end of the war, and we weren't. We certainly paid for that defeat, believe you me! But at last it's over. The war's behind us, dead and buried. We can have mocha cake, new clothes, cars, all the nice things. We're no longer lagging behind the rest of the world. We're a force to be reckoned with from now on."

Indeed, Germany was no longer lagging behind everyone else. And they were intent on making that very clear. In a matter of just a few weeks, Germany had managed to shatter the world political order. The major powers – the USSR, Great Britain and the United States – were weighing up the situation. Molotov, Chamberlain and Churchill spoke out one after the other: they could no longer ignore Germany's provocations.

François, absurdly cheerful, was the perfect host, and kept trying to pull us out of our despair.

"Come on, let's make up some beds in the attic. You'll be comfortable there. And we'll find a bottle of something to celebrate your being here. It's not as though we receive good news very often! Am I right?"

I could only think of one thing: Lili. My little girl, all alone at the worst possible time. I couldn't imagine ever being able to sleep again.

We moved into the attic and slowly began to find our bearings.

Days passed and we kept ourselves informed of the political situation as it gradually worsened. June 1940 was the saddest month of my entire life, with 22 June without doubt the absolute nadir of my gloom. François came upstairs with the newspaper.

"That's it . . . You realize that's the same train carriage, no less, as in 1918? Their chap certainly does have a warped sense of humour . . ."

Hitler wanted to erase the insult of the Treaty of Versailles. The June 1940 armistice was signed, at his insistence, in the same train carriage as the one in which the November 1918 armistice had been agreed. Ever aware of the power of symbols to atone for humiliation, his revenge was complete. We, the veterans, had fought each other for nothing. Life went on. No one had any choice. But this time, it was us who had to go without. Whenever I used my ration card to buy sugar I would think of Ilse. One pound ten ounces of sugar per person per month since 1 June until further notice.

To take my mind off things, and to thank him for offering us a roof over our heads and his protection, I began helping François in the fields. There was no question of living off our relatives' hospitality without giving something back, for we had no idea how long it would be before we could go home. I was learning a little about farming and Hélène began sewing again. One night she spoke to me for the first time since we'd left the north, to tell me she had found a few clients. "I already have a little notebook for my orders."

Weeks dragged by like years, until one lovely July day Lili turned up, looking like a ghost. She was thin, like the rest of us, suffering because of rationing, but she was alive. I shouted with joy when I saw her, the heaviness that had been weighing on me suddenly lifted. I had a daughter! I hadn't lost everything. She flung her arms around me, weeping with joy, and I held her tight. A beautiful moment like this made all the hours of suffering disappear in an instant.

Hélène ran to join our embrace, and we clung to each other, wanting to fill each other to the brim with our love. Lili wiped away her tears and began jumping up and down with excitement, like the little girl she no longer was. She had grown since we'd last seen her. Her face had slimmed down and her expression was more serious. She had become a young woman.

"Guillaume is alive!" she cried.

Hélène stared at her for a moment and then, lightning fast, she slapped her. I tried to grab her hand, but it was too late. She struggled to get free, puce with fury.

"How dare you? You think we're not suffering enough?"

Lili, holding her hand to her cheek, carried on talking as if nothing had happened.

"Eugénie, Ginette's cousin, told me when I was in Paris. He's with Ginette."

We stared at each other for a long moment. It was as if we were in a trance. The news was impossible to take in.

"But he'll be trying to avoid the firing squad," she added under her breath.

"He deserted, you mean?" Hélène muttered through gritted teeth, as if we were being watched.

Loubna, 2005

It was 10 p.m. when Anis knocked at my door. I didn't have to tell him how impatient I was – he knows me better than I know myself. And my impatience was hardly surprising – he was holding a dossier that was going to allow me to find out where I came from.

He put his jacket down on a chair and the fat manila envelope on the coffee table in front of me.

He looked exhausted as he collapsed into the armchair opposite. "Here's all the documentation I've managed to put together. I even stole a few things for you – but don't worry about that. Now you have the letters, though probably not all of them, and some official papers."

He has friends everywhere and always manages to get his way. There was no point in asking how he'd got them. He'd never tell.

"So your grandfather was in the French navy, and after *La Railleuse* blew up, he disappeared."

After that he fell silent, and I realized how afraid I was to dive into these musty old pages that smelled of sorrow.

"Shall I make you a coffee? I—"

Anis interrupted me.

"No don't, I'll do it. I want you to look at this stuff."

I sat down on the sofa in the living room. My fingers were burning. He had stolen documents that were part of my history.

"What possible justification is there for you to steal documents from the navy archives? Do all former marines have to resort to theft to get information?" From the kitchen, Anis explained his thought processes, and the reason he had spent so long getting his hands on the precious documents.

Convinced that my grandfather was German, he'd had no luck gaining access to a whole lot of archives in which anything relating to Guillaume Straub might be found. But eventually he got permission to examine the archives of the French navy.

As I listened to Anis, my fear gradually turned to enormous excitement. Eventually I dared to touch the envelope. I picked it up and opened it, and before I'd even put my hand inside, I suddenly couldn't imagine ever letting it out of my sight. Anis stopped talking for a few moments before returning to my initial question.

"That's what's so troubling, Loubna. There are so many documents that haven't been handed over to people's families. Why has the navy held on to them? It's a mystery."

I was both moved and disturbed to be holding these personal letters belonging to my grandfather, about whom I knew nothing. Anis was still talking about all his efforts, all the bureaucratic twists and turns.

He came back into the living room with two cups of coffee. My stomach was rumbling and I realized I had neither eaten anything all day, nor slept a wink all night.

"When I started looking into it, I thought I'd just find out his identity, a couple of photographs, a few official documents, and that would be it. But I found all this."

"This is incredible, Anis! So much more than I ever hoped for!"

He frowned. He looked like he wanted to say something else, but he held back.

I began looking through this extraordinary gift. I emptied the envelope and distractedly began to flick through its contents: personal correspondence, documents, unsealed envelopes. I touched them lightly with just the tips of my fingers as if they were fragile treasure.

I imagined strange, unlikely tales. The papers in front of me surely contained information that neither my father nor I had ever known, and which would help me understand where I was from.

The documents had been sorted into different packets. Firstly, private correspondence he'd received. Then official documents, copies of letters that had been sent to his relatives, as far as I could see. And finally, a small notebook with his name on the cover, its pages covered with doodles. I held it up and sniffed. It smelled musty. It was sixty-five years old, and I was the first person, apart from Anis and the navy, ever to lay eyes on it.

I opened the first packet, which contained letters. I flicked through the dates and names. Some of the pages were illegible. Time, sea salt and water had smudged whole sections. But I could see some names that reappeared again and again: Lucien, Hélène, Lili. His parents and his sister, all three of whom signed every letter they sent him. I discovered their address. They had lived in the Somme – a region to the north of Paris, I discovered when I checked on a map of France. The correspondence covered the years 1936 to 1940, ending abruptly with his death on 30 March 1940. His ship had blown up.

Other names appeared. Friends, other sailors for the most part. Louis, on duty in Bizerte, in Tunisia. Étienne, who'd stayed at home in the Somme, a childhood friend to whom he wrote largely to discuss Ginette. Felix, a sailor on the same ship as him, who wrote to him from time to time from Toulon to give him news of girls or mutual friends.

And there were letters filled with words of endearment. I didn't want to read them yet. I kept them until last. I wanted to get to know his friends and family before plunging into his love life.

I laid them down in neat piles. My heart was beating so wildly it felt as though my whole chest was throbbing. Ali's dark hints, which had filled my head since the morning, vanished in an instant. I was a little girl again. Tears were rolling down my cheeks, in spite of my huge smile, and I heard myself whisper in a choked voice, "I'm going to find out who my grandmother was!"

Ginette, 1940

When I saw Guillaume at the port in Toulon, he was even more handsome than I remembered. The worry that darkened his eyes only made his brooding looks more intense. Then I saw that he wasn't rushing to greet me like he used to, and I grew afraid. He was so near, and yet so distant at the same time. My eyes filled with tears.

I was carrying a small suitcase and a copy of *Confidences* magazine. I'd bought it for the train journey. It was a long way from the Somme region down to Toulon, and I'd had plenty of time to read and reread it. His sister Lili and I always used to laugh at the desperate letters from women revealing their private lives and asking for advice. One of us would mimic the reader's woes and the other the advice of the journalist, who wrote under the pen name Marie-Madeleine:

My husband comes home late every evening. He smells of another woman's perfume and doesn't even bother to wipe off the lipstick she has left on his neck. What can I do? All I want is to take my children and escape to my sister's, to make him realize the pain he is causing me . . .

As always, Marie-Madeleine preached stoicism and tolerance:

Blaming the separation on your husband will lead you nowhere, and he might leave you for good. You are and must remain his wife – loving, patient and indulgent. As the holy scriptures remind us, you married your husband for better or for worse. He will grow tired of his infidelity. He will come back, I assure you.

Mistresses were also lectured by Marie-Madeleine:

Make the right decision, or you will waste your best years and risk finding yourself alone, or making a woman suffer who does not deserve such betrayal, still less to see her family torn apart. Avoid consorting with married men. Resist such passion, which can only ever end in disaster.

And then there were the young women who reminded us of ourselves:

Gaston has been thrusting himself on me for months, and since we are not married, I have, of course, continued to push him away. But he has just been called up and he wants me to be his. I don't know what to do. I am utterly confused. Should I give in to the man I love, who loves me deeply too, or resist so that I can wait for the day – which may never come – when we are married? Readers of Confidences, *help me. Must I refuse and risk losing him, or give in to the urge that consumes me?*

It goes without saying that Marie-Madeleine and her readers concluded that she must resist at all costs:

A brief moment of pleasure could ruin the rest of your life. A moment of passion is not worth such a sacrifice. If he loves you as much as you appear to think he does, he will wait for you and reward you with consummate happiness: marriage.

Though Lili and I laughed, we knew that our own appetite for love also concealed real anxiety. We were on the cusp of war, and ever since the last one, men were more and more scarce . . . Any woman who got her hands on one was not going to let him go.

I had never had the slightest doubt that my future was with Guillaume. He had loved me and I him as far back as I could remember. But war had turned him into someone I was beginning to no longer recognize. He had seen and done things that had changed him, and each time he left I regretted a little more not having given him what he wanted. Right until the moment I surrendered to him. Especially since I was all too conscious of the growing distance these articles talked about. I couldn't do it. I couldn't bear to give him up, to find myself alone. All the girls were in love with him. My only friend was his sister. Was my fate to have paradise dangled in front of me only to then have it torn away?

Of course, Étienne also had feelings for me, strong ones, and had even made a play for me, betraying his oldest friend. I never told Guillaume. It showed me Guillaume was not my only hope for companionship, but it was him I wanted from the absolute depths of my soul. We had promised ourselves to one another. It was written in the stars.

I thought about the letter he had sent me telling me it was all over. It was so unlike him, but the sudden chill in his expression when he looked at me now was unlike him too. The despair of the readers of *Confidences* had always entertained and amused me. I never imagined that I would feel it too one day, that I would copy their desperate strategies to win over my own sweetheart, do whatever I could to avoid losing him. Guillaume had never shown the slightest coolness before. I was ready to do anything to get him back.

We looked at each other, without embracing. He looked serious, troubled. I had never seen him like that; he always had a mischievous little glint in his eye.

We walked towards the restaurant he always took me to whenever I went to see him. We sat down at a table. I was trembling.

I didn't let him say anything, I was determined to be the first to speak. My words came pouring out, as though a dam had burst and was flooding a plain.

"I'm pregnant. Pregnant with your child, Guillaume . . . I'll follow you wherever you want to go. All the way to Africa, the desert, Casablanca, if that's where you choose."

Loubna, 2005

My mobile beeped and I woke with a start. I was lying down with a blanket over me. I struggled to clear my head of the unsettling dreams I'd had. I had no memory of lying down and falling asleep.

That morning the weather was gorgeous, as it was almost all year round. Bright sunlight reflected off the dirty white façade of the wall facing my window and softly stroked my face. I stretched and listened to the sounds of the city. The rumble of the white beast as it slowly swallowed up the sounds of the night. Silvery particles of dust floated in the rays of sunshine.

I glanced at my phone and saw a message from Ali. "I'd like to see you again. Without Liz. No haunted house. Tomorrow evening at 8 p.m. I'll swing by and pick you up."

I noticed there was no question mark. He didn't seem to expect me to respond, let alone turn him down.

After such a short night, I wasn't in any mood to leap out of bed and make a decision, and I have to admit, in spite of myself, that I quite liked his commanding manner. Even though his tactless comment about my family had been extremely rude, I was still dying to see him again. Beyond the secret he held, there was something seductive about him; a shadowy, irresistible charm.

I made myself a cup of coffee and sat down at the table in front of the documents I'd been engrossed in late into the night.

A short while later Anis turned up with a bottle of chilled *leben*, fermented milk, some lovely-looking oranges and a big bag of delicious cornmeal biscuits made with the olive oil that his grandfather produced in the foothills of the High Atlas mountains, among his rose bushes and argan trees.

"Ah, you're up already? You were sleeping like a log when I left."

I looked greedily at the food on the table. My stomach was rumbling. Twenty-four hours of fasting didn't suit it very well.

"Thank you so much, Anis!"

"Your mother made them this morning, and she saved a few for us. Enjoy."

"A few!" I said with a laugh. "A mountain of them, you mean." Anis squeezed the oranges and served us each a large glass of juice.

My mouth was watering. I sat down and bit into a biscuit. My mother knew the secret of making them crunchy on the outside and meltingly soft inside. The olive oil gave them a fresh, green fragrance, woody and lush, that made me think of mornings when we were children, when Anis and I used to go to Ouarzazate with his family. For two months every summer our eyes no longer gazed on the white walls of Casablanca but on the red earth of Drâa-Tafilalet, where every year we would be awestruck at the first sight of the desert, which we imagined to be as infinite as the sand dunes fashioned by the capricious wind. This was a world where our games were filled with rain-eating monsters, Berber looters, explorers who had lost their way, and djinns who lived in oases deep in the desert.

I often think back fondly to what was generally a very happy childhood. Though I didn't have a father and Anis didn't have a mother, in all other respects we wanted for nothing. Our two slightly lopsided selves leaned on each other, and we offered each other the guidance and love that we lacked. The rest, we picked up randomly from other people in our lives. We never hid anything from each other, until the day I realized I had feelings for Salim, the wild one in his group of friends. I loved how little he seemed to care about serious things. This was the first secret to come between Anis and me, and our first argument. I fell in love, I suffered, then my relationship with Anis went back to what it had been before. Sometimes, after one of the long silences that sometimes arose between us, I would catch him looking at me with a strange expression, a mixture of trepidation and surprise. I didn't know anything about his love affairs, whether fleeting or significant. They took place outside the world he had constructed around me. We were like cats that come back once they've had enough of being stroked.

Anis was already immersed in the documents. I watched as he nibbled a biscuit and took notes. I interrupted his reading.

"Do you realize we never actually used to go into the desert? We always stayed just at the edge of it."

I knew, as he put the papers down, that he too was thinking about us at different ages, remembering the way we used to sit side by side on the little wall behind his grandfather's house, our faces tilted towards the dawn as it set the tawny mountains ablaze. How many times had we stared into the sun, before racing off to seek shelter from the summer heat? Or watched the ocean lapping the Casablanca coastline spread out in cascades of blue-tinted concrete?

The clarity of the horizon washed our vision clean after months roaming the jumble of alleyways that teemed with endless columns of human beings brimming with emotion and faith, their faces aged by the sun and the burden of the city, all smiles and remnants of smiles, murmuring I have nothing, or I have everything; whispering at least I have you or I cannot even weep.

"We'll go there together, Loubna. I promise."

He stood up to pour himself another cup of coffee, perhaps to chase away the thoughts that filled his head. I returned to the subject that had been obsessing me since he'd handed me the envelope.

"I keep thinking, if the navy kept hold of these documents, and examined some of them so closely – here, look . . ."

I handed him some letters full of words obscured by thick black lines, and notes in the margins in red and blue ink. Anis had had plenty of time during his research to familiarize himself with all these papers.

". . . I guess it was because he was . . . how should I put it . . . suspicious?"

I was aware I wasn't telling Anis anything he didn't know, and he nodded. Presumably this was what he'd been hoping to keep me from seeing for a few more hours.

"One might suppose that since war had just broken out, some of the documents might have been overlooked, but I don't think that was the case, Loubna. It's obvious they were carefully examined, read and reread. And if they were kept in the navy archives instead of being returned to his family in France, presumably it's because there was some suspicion surrounding your grandfather's activities . . . and probably also his involvement in the accident."

He had mentioned a premeditated "accident", with his customary tact.

"And then there's the huge amount of cash that your grandmother had on her. Quite an enormous sum for the time – there's no way it came from someone on a navy stipend."

Anis had already done all the research.

"It's just not possible, even if he'd been saving – which I doubt, firstly because he was so young, and secondly because at the time sailors didn't have much to do so they tended to spend their money while they were off duty and on shore leave."

Even without examining the letters in detail, I knew that some fairly significant mystery had pushed the authorities at the time – and over the following decades – to keep the affair under wraps. By now it had most likely been forgotten, and Anis had been able to grease the palm of someone high up in the archives, maybe someone he'd been at university with, so that I could have the documents for a few days.

The historian in Anis dreamed of delving into the history of the major events that had shaken Morocco in 1940 and perhaps were linked in some way to my grandfather.

"Don't forget that Morocco – ergo France as well, because

we were still a protectorate – took advantage of its rear-guard position. For example, tons of gold were hidden in Casablanca when the Nazis began to get dangerously close to Paris. The Bank of France moved it out of the country and stashed it here. And, more generally, after the armistice was signed in June 1940, Morocco found itself between a sovereign state that had just rallied to support the Vichy regime, and the Free French, who had joined forces with the Allies. The navy, specifically, hesitated for a period of time between joining forces with Marshal Pétain or President de Gaulle. You can imagine how this sort of prevarication led to a very delicate situation. No one talks about them now, but did you know there were Nazi concentration camps in Morocco?"

Anis got the reaction he was clearly after: I was utterly astonished, dumbstruck by this extraordinary piece of information that he had dropped so casually into the conversation. He continued, apparently encouraged:

"General Noguès, for example, who was Governor of Morocco at the time, wholeheartedly supported the Vichy regime during the Second World War, and its racist and anti-semitic policies. Of course, later on he joined de Gaulle. But the political and social atmosphere at the time meant there was a lot of shifting of allegiances. So what was your grandfather up to? Did he sense the tide was turning? Did he decide to put his money on a German victory? He did have a German-sounding surname, after all . . . Still, I don't think that's a conclusive argument. It's true that the French and the Germans had already waged plenty of wars against each other, but they were also bordering countries with a lot of trade between them. Having said that, his name could have been enough to turn him into the black sheep of the navy."

He shifted his chair and moved closer to me to show me the documents that he had been reading during the night.

"I've gone through all the official papers. There's no death certificate. His body was never recovered."

Anis's historical rationality contrasted radically with my

romantic and fraught reading of the documents. I told myself that the truth was somewhere in between.

"So basically he was either a traitor or a deserter," Anis concluded bluntly.

"Right. Wow. What an inheritance."

I lowered my eyes, more than a little disappointed that my grandfather had not been a heroic figure who'd distinguished himself with peerless acts of bravery. I had been preparing myself to accept that he had been a coward; but a spy, a traitor . . . these were words that were strangely painful.

"And then there is one other possible explanation."

"I'm listening."

"He did die on the ship in the explosion, and for some reason that we will doubtless never discover, his body was never found . . . But that he should have made everyone suspect him of betrayal, pretending to have been offered the perfect opportunity to escape unharmed into the desert with his sweetheart, alias your grandmother, no less . . . that would be one hell of an irony."

My mobile beeped – I had a new message. Anis and I both looked at it. It was Ali again:

"Wear something nice. I'm taking you somewhere rather chic."

I felt my cheeks redden. Anis noticed. He didn't say anything, merely turned back to the letter he was reading, frowning as if it were a riddle that would never be solved.

III

Misunderstandings

Felix, 1940

I had enough time to take Lili down to my sister's place in Toulouse, where she lived with her husband and two children. We hadn't seen each other for a long time. My heart was heavy when I set off again, alone. My God, I loved Lili so much! I wanted to get back on a ship about as much as I wanted to hang myself. I hardly even knew her, but already I cared for her more than anything else in the world!

I didn't even wait till I got back to Toulon to write to her. I told her things I didn't know I was capable of saying, but the words came without any prompting. I cried like a baby as I wrote them. My eyes were so blurry with tears that from time to time I had to wipe them away to stop the ink smudging.

> *I can't think of anyone but you. I know you know, Liliane, how fond your brother was of me. He wanted to be able to protect you, but now it's me who wants to protect you, from war, violence and death. Wait for me.*

Bloody hell! I thought talking about love was just for starry-eyed girls swooning at the pictures, goggle-eyed at stars like Arletty, Michèle Morgan and Mireille Balin. Wishing they too were up on screen, dreaming of a glamorous life . . . But here I am, just as bewitched, so I can't scoff at all that stuff any more. I want to see her, I can't help myself . . . I've got it bad.

I can't stop thinking what a lucky bastard I am. God, I hope it lasts. When I think of how many friends in the army and the air force I've lost . . . It's been wholesale slaughter. Absolute devastation. It's nothing like that when you're in the navy. Even

when the ships blew up, I somehow managed to be far away
. . . Right now, I'm stuck in Toulon waiting to hear what ship
I'm assigned to, spending my time writing love letters that
probably look totally daft to anyone who's never felt like this.

That kiss we had on the train has been going round my
head on a loop; it made me so happy, and it broke my heart
at the same time. And now I've started talking like Guillaume
. . . Who'd have thought it! Even when she was pouring her
heart out to me in Paris, she was so dignified . . . Her hair was
so neat, in a perfect marcel wave with that little kiss-curl on
her forehead, all glossy . . . The scent of her when we were on
the train . . . Somehow I managed to put out of my mind how
much classier she is than me . . . and then she didn't even push
me away – I couldn't believe it!

I'm feeling so responsible for her now that I'm more uneasy
than ever thinking about what happened with her brother, that
friend in Paris who told her he'd run off with Ginette . . . In
the moments when I can drag my thoughts away from Lili, I
remember Guillaume the last time I saw him, a few hours
before the explosion.

The more I think about it, the more I remember all the stuff
that doesn't quite add up, especially since we found out about
him doing a bunk with a pretty girl. Guillaume had changed,
we'd all noticed. His expression was different. We'd teased him
a bit, said things like, "What are you on the lookout for,
you old dog? Your next conquest?" We'd all noticed how he'd
stopped staring at the horizon, how he kept his eyes fixed on
the quay. He literally turned his back on the Mediterranean.

A couple of years ago, when we found out we'd both been
assigned to Casablanca on the same ship, both of us were
pleased as punch to have a friend on board. It was his ticket
to a new horizon, and his eyes sparkled at the thought. But
just a few weeks ago, that light went out. Then he started
surveying people from the guardrail up on the poop deck. Now
I understand why: he must have been looking out for his girl.

He'd stand there for hours, watching, a cigarette hanging

out of his mouth. Leaning on the guardrail, he'd look at all the people walking by – women mostly, I think – as if there might be someone special hiding down there. It was like the sea had no hold over him any more.

He no longer even looked at it. The weather was absolutely beautiful. It was the end of April, and by then in Morocco it's like full summer in northern Europe. Even so, he kept his eyes on the city. I have to say it's not easy to keep dreaming with the war taking up all your attention. It was pretty much all we talked about, and however we might cross our fingers that it wouldn't spread, it felt a bit like a high wall had gone up all of a sudden, blocking our view of the horizon. In Morocco it was like everyone thought the war was happening far away, and we were fretting for nothing – our troops would snuff it out before it really took hold. Bloody fools.

Anyway, I was sure that what I was seeing was fear. I thought that was what had put out the light in his eyes, that was why he was so down in the dumps. And then a few days, or a few weeks, maybe, before the explosion, I saw her, the girl he'd been waiting for all this time. She started coming nearly every day. The other night I woke up with a start, as if the devil himself had paid me a visit. It wasn't the devil, but the memory of the moment I left the ship for the last time. Like a nightmare, I had a flashback, so clear, so distinct . . . It gave me goose-pimples. Guillaume was on the bridge, and as I walked past him, I tapped him on the shoulder, and we exchanged a few words. As usual he was looking out for his lady friend to show up. As I jumped out onto the dock, I saw her, faithful as ever, standing there on the quay, and I don't know why but I instinctively turned round. I gave him a wink and a little wave. He responded with a big grin. And then I saw him glance to the right. He froze suddenly, stopped smiling . . . He wasn't looking cheerful any more. But I didn't let it distract me from the hours of amusement ahead; I set off into town to forget the wretched sea.

That was the last time I ever saw him. His last words keep

coming back to me like a punch in the face. They fill my dreams, and I don't even know what they meant.

They're the kind of words whose deeper meaning escapes you. They go round and round in your head, and eventually they do you in.

"Have fun, Felix! I've got some things to sort out. I can't take leave right now."

Ginette, 1940

My heart was beating furiously and in an instant I'd said the unthinkable.

There had been one reader's letter in *Confidences* that had deeply moved me:

> *I loved Pierre with all my heart, and when he told me he was about to go off to war, I wasn't able to fight my fear. I made the mistake of giving in to him and now I'm paying for my weakness. I'm pregnant. When I told him, I was sure he would tell me he loved me as much as I loved him. But no, he refuses to hear anything more from me or to acknowledge his daughter. What should I do?*

She gave me an idea. I would tell Guillaume I was pregnant. He'd been in love with me since we were children. The date of our last meeting tallied. I could always tell him later that I'd lost the baby. Who would know? Perhaps I really would fall pregnant. In any case, I knew, I was sure, he wouldn't leave me after that. He was a man who kept his promises, not a little boy who took fright at the slightest setback. He'd wanted to go to sea – that was proof of his courage. He was a man who was always one step ahead of his desires, and I knew I was among them. When he'd enlisted he'd sworn to me that he would come back and marry me. I was simply accelerating the process. My tears of desperation – I felt so cruelly abandoned – made my announcement seem even more credible.

I didn't think beyond that. I don't know why or how I told him. The words came out of my mouth almost in spite of myself. But once I had uttered them, it was difficult to take them back.

Guillaume reacted terribly badly. I didn't recognize him. I was like that pathetic girl who'd written to *Confidences*. But at least she hadn't lied, she really was carrying the child of the man she loved. My dishonesty prevented me from fighting back, and the callousness of his reaction took my words and my breath away. He left me at the port as I'd arrived: sad, alone, in tears, enduring constant wolf whistles from passing sailors. I spent the night weeping in the hotel where we once used to make love.

After a broken, dreamless night, I got up to a new day. I didn't see my life in the same way any more. Not only had the fighting spread, but it was no longer just between men. Now men and women were battling for a corner of blue sky among all the chaos. And Guillaume had no idea how far I was prepared to go to avenge myself for this terrible rejection.

Loubna, 2005

Judging from the censor's marks scored all over my grand-father's correspondence, it's impossible not to think he must have had something on his conscience. He had clearly raised suspicions in other people's minds. The letters were covered in red and blue lines. His privacy had been violated by the hand of some military pen-pusher whose purpose was to harm the grandfather whose handwriting I'd not yet seen, because here were only letters he had received and none in his own hand.

Following Anis's suggestion, I went through the letters in reverse, which made me feel like I was retracing my own history. A bureaucratic communication dated April 1940 – in other words a few days after the disaster – stated impersonally that the letters had been found in a suitcase identified as having belonged to Guillaume Straub. The suitcase was found floating on the surface of the sea, which had prevented water from getting inside and explained why they were so well preserved. My heart was thumping as I contemplated the pile of documents that contained the truth.

There were letters from his relatives, a few additional documents, appendices, copies of letters sent to the family (including a copy of a letter from Captain Hourcade), requests from the family for his body to be repatriated, details of the pension they would receive as the family of someone who had "died for his country" . . .

Angry strokes underlined passages that had apparently appeared suspicious to the reader. I quickly skimmed through the letters, taking care not to damage the faded sheets of paper, which had become brittle with the passage of time.

I started with the letters from his relatives and friends. First, those from his family, then the ones from his girlfriends. A lot of different women had written to my grandfather between 1936 and 1940. A little surprised, I sorted them into piles. The more I went through them, the more there seemed to be. Dozens of women had written to him, long letters, short letters, letters filled with love and invective in equal measure, sheets of paper densely covered in handwriting that was sometimes tentative, sometimes so forceful that the paper had torn.

I was beginning to piece together what kind of a man he must have been. He was clearly a collector of conquests. Filled with curiosity, I began to read.

Guillaume,

    You have brought sunlight into my grieving heart. I know you were a dear friend to Bastien. You assured me my beloved brother did not suffer – a sentence I would never have imagined bringing me such comfort. I grieve for him, but knowing he would not have been aware he was about to die is all that matters. That and the thought of seeing you again. Your mouth on mine allowed me briefly to forget this nightmare, wiped the recurring images of the explosion of the Pluton *briefly from my mind.*

    We shall see each other again in a few days, and I can barely stand the wait. Fate brought you knocking at my door. The sun has shone less brightly on Marseille since you left. You are the only person who will ever make me smile again, and chase the ghastly horrors from my mind. Guillaume, I am waiting for you, and I know you are waiting for me as well.

    Nelly

I jotted down the name of each correspondent in a little notebook. One of them must surely have been my grandmother. I assumed, to begin with, that she must be the one who wrote most often or at least the most ardently.

My darling, my beloved,

It was too short. How I wish we could have stayed together forever. Write and tell me when you are next on leave and I shall come and meet you. I'll say I'm going to visit my cousin in Paris. I've let her know; she'll cover for me and won't say a word to anyone. I'm writing on the train back to the Somme region, and I'm filled with melancholy. The smell of you is still on my skin. Were you telling me the truth when you told me you loved me, and that this love is what will get you through the war? I dare to believe you. Because the promise of happiness is what will enable me too to endure the coming war. I'm so afraid. My parents are talking of going south, they say they have to be prepared to leave at any moment. If the Germans manage to break through the Maginot Line, they will take Paris, and northern France will surely not be spared. We'll probably be the first to face the armies of the Reich. I'm scared, but I know you are mine, and that gives me the strength to get through this.

My love, we've only just said goodbye and I cannot wait to see you again.

Ginette

PS. I don't know if I will be able to come to meet you in Casablanca. Things are incredibly tense now. We may have to wait till everything is over. I will come to Toulon as soon as you are next on leave.

Another name for my list. Then there were passionate letters from Paulette and Louise. From Claudette, promising him that her husband won't burst in "like the last time . . . What a panic, thinking back to that moment." Janine was apparently ready to ditch everything – Marseille and the beginnings of a not very promising career: "Life in the colonies rather appeals to me. I'm sure I'll find an audience in the dance halls of Casablanca . . . Oh Guillaume, I can already picture us there, our lovely new life. It'll be smashing!" Nicole, on the other hand, either out of instinct or experience, wrote him a letter of farewell: "I know you sailors. You're nothing but a charming mirage. Off you go on your adventures – your promises aren't worth the paper they are written on. Have a nice life."

I was a little surprised to discover my grandfather's success with women; it was an unexpected character trait.

As I delved deeper into these love letters, I noticed a change of tone as time went on.

Amiens

My darling, my beloved,

You've changed. I don't want to bother you with my doubts, but you seemed very different. I could tell that your thoughts kept wandering, and I think I know why. You're afraid. War is looming. The Germans are getting closer. We thought the Poles were strong enough to push them back, but that wasn't the case. We shall have to go to their aid. And now the Belgians have surrendered. We're afraid, but we can't afford to get caught up in another war that will cost us heavily in lives and hope. We shall have to get it over with, and with brave men like you I'm confident we will. I'm sure the war won't drag on and the worst will be avoided.

I think of you all the time, with sadness and melancholy, but always with affection. We'll be together again soon, and you won't have anything to occupy your mind except the love we have for each other, and nothing else to do but bring our dreams to life. The little house with a garden, a vegetable patch, and our children playing happily.

I love you.

Come back to me.

Ginette

Marseille

Guillaume,

I don't understand your letter. You sound so cold and hard. Did you really write it? Did someone force you to reply to me like that, with such unkindness? That's the only explanation I can think of, because I don't recognize you anywhere in those words.

I read that the Pluton *blew up in the port of Casablanca, right next to your ship. I suppose you must have been friends with the sailors on board. You must be crazed with fear and feelings of helplessness, but I beg you not to give up now. Life will go on, with me by your side.*

Come back to me. Come back to me and I will forget everything. This woman you're talking about is just a moment of madness, I know she is. I'll forget all about it.

Ginette

Guillaume,

How you have changed. You're not the person you were when we met. What's happened to you? What's happened to the charming man who made me so happy?

War certainly does make men behave badly. As if we women weren't suffering enough! We have to put up with everything without complaining because you are the ones fighting. But that's not really true. Since my brother died and my father left, it's just me, looking after my mother and my sister. It's a real struggle to make ends meet, and believe me, there's often as great a distance between these two ends as the one between your promises and your actions!

I never want to see you again. Go to hell.

Agathe

Guillaume,

You'll pay for this. The tears I shed in the train from Toulon to Amiens are the last tears I will ever shed for you.

You don't deserve them. You are not Étienne. He knows the
love of a woman must be earned; he doesn't try to shirk his
responsibilities like some kind of petty criminal.

Go to hell! The next time you have news of me, you'll
have heard it from someone else, and you'll be sorry for
every single word you said. You don't deserve the love I
had for you. And now you're nothing to me. You're dead
to me.

Adieu
Ginette

I was stunned. Not only because the letters conjured a past
that had been hidden from me, but also because I couldn't get
away from the fact that a few weeks or months before the
explosion, my grandfather had completely changed. Something
had clearly been going on. He'd begun acting in a horribly
sleazy manner.

Out of the blue, I was now privy to my grandfather's personal
life and I began to suspect he had been harbouring a shameful
secret. I found myself getting to know a man who made me
extremely uneasy. I was seeing him only through the words of
various jilted women, while being in the privileged position
of knowing that however spineless he might have been, none
of them ever retaliated.

"What were you expecting, Loubna?" Fatimah asked. I had
gone round to see her, somewhat bemused by the turn my
search for my roots had taken.

I needed to talk to someone who was both more objective
than I could be, and had a sense of humour, and I knew that
I could count on Fatimah for both.

"The truth is I just don't see anything of myself in him . . ."

She gave me a long, hard look, and then began to laugh, as
if she'd never heard anything so ridiculous in her entire life.
Which is exactly when I realized what I'd been hoping for:
to see myself in him, to hear him speaking in my words, my
voice, as if he'd bequeathed me a major part of his character,

preferably his most admirable qualities. As if our blood connection would be incontrovertibly revealed by a number of shared characteristics, obvious from the very first glance.

Fatimah kept giggling at me, at what she called my naïvety.

"The situation is very straightforward, Loubna. First of all, he's a man. Secondly, he's barely even twenty. Thirdly, he's a sailor. Fourthly, he's been to a lot of exotic countries . . ." She stopped, her four fingers pointing to the sky, tangible witnesses to my stupidity.

I looked at her, baffled. She went on.

"What more do you need to make someone a sexual obsessive? It's like leaving a hungry wolf alone inside a butcher's shop. He's going to help himself. And then on top of that, remember, he must have spent long periods at sea with only men for company. And sometimes he would have been risking his life . . . That would have given him plenty to brag about once he was on shore leave. Come on, Loubna, you know what men are like . . ."

At this point her husband, Karim, walked into the room. He sat down beside her and put his arm around her shoulders, smiling. He was never happier than when she was analysing situations with her legendary bluntness, always using lots of unexpected metaphors.

"Fatimah told me – it's exciting, everything you're finding out, Loubna. You're bound to find all the pieces of the puzzle are in a bit of a jumble. When you think about it, we've been hearing about this for – how long now? It's twenty years since we first met."

They looked at each other. Fatimah and Karim had been together forever. Anis had introduced us all to each other when we were teenagers, and our weekly rendezvous at the Rialto were set in stone. Right from the start, we knew they would get together, just like in the movies. As if Karim had read my thoughts, he steered the conversation down a more serious path.

"You know, life isn't like a film, Loubna. Life is what happens before the reel starts up, and after it's finished turning. It's everything leading up to the poetic moments and everything that comes after. You can't avoid it forever."

"What can I say, Karim . . . I can't stop myself trying to find those poetic moments, even when they're hidden – that just makes them more beautiful."

I finished my tea; it had brewed too long and tasted bitter. I tried to work out what was bothering me.

"You're right. But still, there does seem to be something slightly amiss . . . It's true that he doesn't come across at all how I imagined him, to put it mildly. But he's my grandfather, his blood is in my veins, that's the thing . . . And now I have a real problem – I have a ton of possible grandmothers!"

The doorbell rang – it was Anis, come to see Karim. They were rehearsing for a concert the following day. Karim was the singer, who layered his melodious voice over the rhythm of Anis on the *djembe*.

Anis looked surprised. He hadn't been expecting to see me here; for months I'd been avoiding their weekly practice. Salim was about to turn up. He was always late. He'd come through the door, his guitar on his back and his skateboard under his arm. Seeing him was bound to upset me, but for the first time since we'd split up, that didn't worry me. He was a bit like a sailor too, in a way, with a woman in every port. And I had been one of them, though never the favourite. But since Anis had brought up the possibility of tracing my grandfather, I hadn't given Salim a moment's thought.

I'd needed this conversation with Fatimah, and it was worth risking another crack in my broken heart.

Without addressing a word to me, Anis turned to Karim and said, "Let's go, we've got a lot to get through tonight."

They shut themselves up in the office at the end of the corridor, and Fatimah gave me a quizzical look, trying to work out what had caused this sudden coolness between Anis and me. I realized he hadn't been behaving normally since Ali's text. That must have been why he was in a bad mood.

"I'm seeing Ali tomorrow evening, and I think he's not too happy about it," I whispered.

Fatimah sprang to her feet and grabbed her denim jacket and handbag.

"I'm coming with you," she said. "I want to see these letters, photos . . . and Ali," she called back, already in the corridor. "You have to tell me everything."

We walked up towards Alger Street, Fatimah hanging on my every word. She knew who Ali was and, like every straight Moroccan woman under forty, she was fascinated by the man who embodied the quintessence of sex appeal in this country: success, charisma and mystery.

We stopped at one of the most dangerous junctions in the city, where the traffic was at its most dense and perilous. It was impossible to understand how the traffic remained fluid, starting and stopping around the gigantic roundabout where cars, trucks and scooters launched themselves into the fray and refused to give way even an inch.

Each lost in our own thoughts, the two of us stood still for a moment, hypnotized by the perpetual ballet of colour and scraping metal.

Fatimah raised her voice over the concerto of car horns. "Look at that, Loubna. The cars are practically crashing – they're only just missing each other. I don't know how they do it, manage to avoid a fatal collision at the last minute and then throw themselves back into that weird sort of laid-back rush-hour waltz."

She stopped, then said, "I don't know why, but you meeting Ali, it's suddenly made me see erotic images all the time! Even the way the taxis move around each other, can you believe it? Anyway, tell me what he was wearing – I want more details . . ."

As we walked up my street, we were overcome by a fit of giggles that grew even more intense as we climbed the stairs to my apartment. All of a sudden Fatimah stopped, and without waiting to catch her breath, she said, "Do you like him, Loubna?

I mean, do you really like him? Because I know someone who's going to kick himself . . ."

Fatimah wasn't asking, she was confirming. She looked at me, trying to gauge my reaction, when my mother, alerted by all the noise we were making, opened her front door and saved me from my blushes. I was aware that I couldn't and shouldn't ask myself that very question Fatimah had just asked. The whole thing with Ali had started off on the wrong footing. I kept thinking about the way he'd told me what he knew. What if he was playing me? I did want to see him again, but every time I thought about our meeting, I felt a kind of dread, like the shadow of a hand on my throat.

"We're just popping home for a minute, Mama!"

Inside the apartment, Fatimah discovered the extent of the task ahead of me.

"Okay, babe, let's get going on these letters. I'm dying to know what he was really like, this ladykiller. Do you reckon he was as charismatic as Humphrey Bogart in *Casablanca*? 'We'll always have Paris'," she declaimed with extravagant solemnity.

I giggled. I was so pleased she was there, with her detachment that helped diffuse my intense emotional engagement, both when it came to the letters and my imminent date with Ali.

I thought back to the film that's been a part of my life forever, since my father used to hum the song to me during the first weeks of my life. I thought of the legendary scene where the two lovers bid each other farewell, Ingrid Bergman on the brink of tears, Humphrey Bogart unruffled, ineffably elegant, even as he's utterly devastated by the laws of fate working against him.

After a long silence, Fatimah raised her eyes from her reading: "The thing that bothers me most is the change of behaviour they all talk about. Just before the accident that killed him, he became incredibly unpleasant. He cut off contact with everyone. There has to be a reason for that."

Felix, 1940

The truth is we all had the feeling he'd got himself caught up in something he couldn't control. He was on edge all the time, observing all the men around him, eyeballing us as if we were either the solution, or a major problem he wasn't going to be able to put off dealing with forever. I'd always thought I knew him quite well, but he was still a bit of a mystery. Back then I didn't really think about it, didn't ask any questions, it was just who he was. He wasn't an ordinary bloke, and he didn't have an ordinary life.

At the end of May, while I was on leave, all, or almost all, the French torpedo ships headed north. The Krauts were coming at us from every direction and it was our job to protect the coast. Their air force was smashing buildings with anti-torpedo ammo. And the whole time, all I could think of was Lili.

She was never not in my thoughts. It was driving me mad, but the good thing about it was that I wasn't so aware of what was going on around me, how quickly the country was falling to the Germans.

Around the end of May, beginning of June maybe, I was put on guard duty in Toulon before being sent back to Casablanca.

And when I got back there, boy were things tense.

I admit I didn't really know what I'd find, but I definitely hadn't been expecting quite such a bloody mess. I'd missed it all first time round, when I'd been caught up in the chaos of the Straubs leaving home for the south. Not this time. "This is History starting, I'm telling you," said Gaston, the owner of the restaurant where we used to go during basic training.

You have to understand the context to see why History went down the pan, pardon the expression. We'd all been on high alert. First there was the *Pluton*, then war was declared, there were manoeuvres galore, we hardly ever got to go ashore for a bit of a breather . . . We didn't know which way to turn, and it was still early days – we'd never fought in a war before. Our fathers, for those of us lucky enough to have one, had talked about the terrible slaughter in the trenches, and there was nothing cheerful in either these old stories or all the new ones. Hitler had brought the Poles to their knees, the Belgians had given up, the Finns had got their backsides kicked hard, the Swedes had decided not to take part . . . The Germans were charging right towards us and nothing and no one could slow them down even a little bit; basically, it was happening all over again. We had this grim sense of *déjà vu*, and this time we were right in the thick of it. We were all at sea, and not only literally.

There were still a few idiots around harping on about the Maginot Line, though there were fewer and fewer of them every day. You should've heard them a month earlier: "The Krauts won't be able to get over the Ardennes. Their tanks won't make it! We'll ambush them higher up. We'll have 'em, you'll see!"

That was the kind of rubbish people were coming out with – no more reassuring than it was helpful. I'd missed Casablanca, the friends who'd left, and the people who knew us when we went ashore to prop up the bars and while away our free time.

So I decided to go and see some mates who'd been wounded and were holed up at the military hospital in Ben M'sik. Blimey, what a welcome. I didn't even need to ask what was going on. While I'd been on leave, I'd missed all the gossip about Guillaume – none of it good – and they were still at it, like dogs with a bone.

I showed up with a big grin on my face.

"All right then, how's things, you lucky buggers who made it off *La Railleuse*?"

There I was thinking we were going to have a bit of a laugh

about it, just between us, but no bloody way! They bent my ear so far it almost fell off. They tore strips off me for having been mates with a "traitor" and a "spy", and a whole load more slurs I won't even bother to list.

I kept my mouth shut about what I'd heard in Paris, obviously. Better off keeping my cards close to my chest.

"Come off it, lads! It's me, Felix! You know perfectly well – I'm so naïve, if it weren't for the fact naïvety was being handed out for free, I'd never have grabbed such a big portion when I was born!"

They lightened up a bit at that, and began to talk more calmly.

While I was gone, they told me, in the days following the explosion on *La Railleuse*, things had got really tense . . . There was a lot of talk, everyone had a story to tell about Guillaume. Especially Marcel. There was some bone of contention between them that went back to something that had happened a long time ago, something to do with a girl. Marcel had ended up with a black eye and he'd kept his distance from Guillaume after that. He was having a field day now, boiling with anger. He told me he'd been thinking about it a lot; he was wound up tight as a spring. He went through the whole story from beginning to end, and when he'd finished he began all over again, but this time the other way round.

"Gotta say, Felix, it all makes sense . . . His surname, Straub. He was obviously German. In his soul, anyway," he added, tapping his chest.

I didn't think that necessarily followed. But everyone else seemed to think it was some kind of proof, suddenly. I'd always known he understood German. There was this one time we managed to persuade Guillaume the Great to come to Bousbir with us. I remember, we'd been stuck in Casablanca for weeks. There was nothing going on, no orders, no wind – not even the faintest fart of a breeze . . . It was the summer of 1938, and there was nothing to do except stare out to sea and go ashore as often as we could.

We were gagging for a bit of action, and at the same time we dreaded it. The war hadn't started yet, but things were beginning to kick off all over the place. So, to chase away the dark thoughts we went out together one evening, four or five of us, in the red-light district; there was a nice little fleapit there, with an open-air screen. We saw a film. We weren't really paying a whole load of attention, I have to admit; we'd had a few beers and were a bit blotto. It was a German flick, *The Blue Angel*. It could have been funnier, I thought. But as always, we put politics aside and concentrated on Marlene Dietrich, pinning our ears back to try and hear the chap by the screen who was translating. I can see us now, trying to make out what he was saying and then looking quickly back at the screen to figure out what was going on. After a bit I glanced over at Guillaume, and saw he wasn't paying the slightest bit of attention to the translator; he was even – get this! – murmuring some of the lines in German.

I didn't say anything about what I'd seen, not to him or anyone else. In fact, I didn't really know what to think. But not for one second, even after war was declared, did I think he'd use it against us now Germany was the enemy. Even after I'd caught him in the act like that, I told myself – yet again – it was simply because he was such a know-it-all.

But Marcel wouldn't let it go. Lying there on his camp bed, which squeaked every time he moved, he was completely obsessed.

"You knew him pretty well – didn't you ever wonder? Course it was him. He sold us down the river, he betrayed us, didn't he? He was a spy in the pay of the Germans."

Maurice had his arm in plaster. He interrupted Marcel to point out that Guillaume was the French for Wilhelm, the name of the last king of Prussia.

"You remember, when it all went belly up at Sarajevo?" he said.

For them, betrayal was an ideology, and this was all they needed to prove it was all Guillaume's fault.

Anyway, I realized that all his old mates had begun to piece together an image of Guillaume that was quite different to the man I knew – this Guillaume was a conman who'd harboured such hatred towards France that he'd joined up to trick us, to avenge his real ancestors, the Teutons, for the insult of the Treaty of Versailles.

The two of them kept yakking on, working themselves into a right lather.

"He must have been stirred into patriotism when he read Hitler's speeches – all that nationalism and stuff."

"I'm positive he swore allegiance to the Führer when he was last on leave – it was only a few weeks before the *Pluton* blew up. It's obvious that's what happened."

Everyone had his own pet theory. It was all mad; there were as many conjectures as there were men. But I was pretty sure that if I said anything at all in his defence, I'd face the firing squad. So I listened, and tried as hard as I could to keep a cool head and remember everything I knew about Guillaume, and all the things I'd been thinking about over the last few days and weeks. We'd been right there when the *Pluton* blew up. And it was right around then that he'd started to change. But obviously we never suspected anything; we were all a bit shaken up by the idea it could have been us, and at moments like that it's easy to be distracted by the fear in your gut.

I'd been so sure they'd find Guillaume's body, and the whole episode would be over; there'd be an explanation and that would be it . . . time to turn the page. End of story.

Admittedly there were a few things that didn't make sense, from what they said. The girl, for example. I was surprised when Marcel mentioned her. It turned out he'd spotted her too, ages ago.

"She was waiting for him, and she wasn't just after a screw, you know what I'm saying, Felix? It made me laugh. I thought she must have sniffed that something was up, or she was absolutely smitten, to be buzzing around him like a fly, given she'd just spent several days with him."

It was obvious when I thought about it – if I'd noticed something, the others were bound to have noticed as well. Marcel was stuck in his hospital bed, legs dead from not moving; he had to keep himself busy somehow . . . So he lay there, wittering on and on. He obviously had these thoughts that kept going round and round his head and he couldn't shut up, kept muttering all kinds of things that I wouldn't say to myself even under my breath.

"She was a spy, that girl of his. He never gave a toss about any of us. It was just a cover, Felix."

His eyes were bloodshot and he was practically shouting. I had no idea what to say.

I forced myself to laugh, to try and lighten the atmosphere.

"Come on, Marcel, he'd have made the worst spy in the world. You'd have to be a real halfwit to get blown up along had the ship when you knew in advance it was going to happen."

But the fact that his body hadn't been found didn't exactly work in his favour. I'd gone round all the hospitals and clinics in Casablanca, asked people who might have seen something, searched every bar and *hôtel de passe* where the whores ply their trade. No trace of Guillaume, alive or dead. Nothing. *Nada.* There'd been no sighting of a six-foot sailor at the Ben M'sik hospital, neither had the body of one turned up at the cemetery in the past few weeks. Even if he'd been swimming with the fishes down in Davy Jones' locker, however famished they were, a great big bloke like that would have had to float to the surface eventually.

We'd counted and recounted the bodies. The only one who didn't respond to the call – for the living or the dead – was Guillaume. And the girl had vanished too. It was all that was needed for the most outlandish stories to flourish. I was convinced he'd made it out somehow, forgotten his service number – he could have been anywhere in Casablanca. Maybe he'd lost his memory. I liked this thought a lot better than the idea of him being a spy who'd coolly planned the attack.

The more I listened to Marcel, the more memories surfaced, and the less straightforward it all seemed. I decided to keep quiet about what I knew: if there was one flaw I couldn't be accused of, it was backstabbing my mates. Anyway, it was better that way, because the more I thought about it the more damning I realized it all was.

At some point Marcel mentioned one last thing that shut me up completely.

"And did you know he wasn't even old enough to enlist in the navy? How many lads like that do you know, who talk all nice, all educated, read books, who are in such a hurry to get their hands dirty for their country?"

Lucien, 1940

The minute I signed the letter I knew I had just suffered my
greatest defeat, because it meant my son would be able to enlist
in the navy. The blackmail had become unbearable and he had
won. He went off to Toulon for basic training, and now every
time he came home on leave the unease between us intensified.

I didn't try to talk him out of it – I was too mortified, too
used to letting the passage of time do its work, too exhausted
by life. I told myself that this too would pass, like everything
else. His sudden hatred towards me would mellow, he would
understand me for who I was. He would forgive me, and he
would never say a word to his mother or to Lili; I wasn't too
worried about that. I knew that the idea of hurting his sister,
and above all his mother, would have horrified him.

It was the beginning of a months-long campaign against me.
What I had first taken as youthful rebellion became a fight to
the death as he raged against my double life. I had long taken
refuge in the belief that I was most myself with the women
with whom I conducted affairs. Since my return from the front
I had been haunted by my memories of the trenches, and I
stumbled upon a kind of oblivion in the arms of these women.
I discovered that there were quite a few women ready to forget
their marriage vows in exchange for the promise of a few hours
of human warmth, or maybe, who knows, the status of a legit-
imate wife in the long run. I never intended to abandon my
family. I was more bound to it than I was to my own self. But
I was sure I'd been successfully concealing my double life. I'd
thought I was being rather cunning, and was terrified of Hélène
finding out.

The thing I had admired in Hélène from the very beginning was her strength. She could have moved mountains. She spent the war years alone, enduring life without me in munitions factories, tirelessly assembling deadly missiles, day and night. We had married in haste – war had just been declared and I wanted her to be safe from hunger or destitution if the situation were to arise. I was somewhat comforted by the thought that if I died it would not be entirely in vain. My conviction that war was imminent hastened my resolve to marry this woman, whom I admired more than I loved.

I was well aware – she had made it clear on multiple occasions – that my survival depended on her rather than the other way around. She wouldn't hesitate to leave me if she found out that I wasn't worthy of her, of her silence, of the promise we had made each other.

Meanwhile Guillaume had been secretly following me and spying on my trysts with the women I had chosen for my hours of distraction.

It began with Agathe. I thought it was a pastime he was bound to tire of, and I decided not to worry about it. This beauty, whom he pursued ardently for several weeks, eventually gave in. Perhaps she concluded that a young man would be a better bet than a married man. One day, at the hour of our weekly rendezvous, she did not answer the door. I heard voices coming from the garden behind her house. I walked round and saw my son cavorting with her; she looked like she was very much enjoying his amorous attentions. The tone of her voice and her peals of laughter reminded me of the first time she and I had made love. I turned round and left. But later that evening, back at home, Guillaume drew me aside.

"You took us quite by surprise earlier." He was toying with an apple, very pleased with himself, full of self-satisfaction. He barely glanced at me. He was trying to back me into a corner.

"I'm fairly sure she prefers youthful passion. You know she

complimented me on my experience? But I'm not interested in her any more. You can have her. You can explain."

I didn't respond to the laugh that punctuated his declaration like a full stop.

I wasn't angry with him. A part of me was even rather proud of him. I'd come across so many men who struggled with their anxieties, who suffered terribly in their interactions with women. At least my son wasn't going to have any problems on that front, I thought to myself that day. I was sure our spat was finally over.

But of course that was merely an opening sally. Guillaume was planning a far more dazzling and inevitably more painful retaliation.

I first met Clotilde in a café in Paris after seeing her perform the leading role in a play. She was married to an English aristocrat, a wealthy businessman, and it was rather a challenge to seduce her, given that she was not actually on the lookout for another man in her life. Her husband had bestowed her with a title and provided her with everything she needed. And far from being content with being supported by her husband, she also had a brilliant career as an actress.

I often used to go to Paris to meet up with the factory's clientele. I liked to make the most of it and often went to the theatre to see a play in the evening. I had begun spending time with influential and wealthy people, who had introduced me into their social circle. I had gone in search of money, and knew where it was to be found; by mimicking their way of life I must have appeared to be the kind of person who belonged in that world.

At the time Clotilde used to appear regularly in the gossip columns. I had never missed even a minor performance of hers. She was superb, captivating on stage, and proved incandescent in our lovemaking. I was consumed by passion, by the radiance of her chestnut hair and storm-grey eyes. If ever a woman had put the tranquillity of my family at risk, it was her. And without me realizing, Guillaume had found out about our dalliance and was determined to make trouble.

One evening after the performance, Clotilde and I met up near Concorde Square, in a discreet little café on a side street close to the theatre. Suddenly, out of nowhere, my son appeared and, as if it were the most natural thing in the world, he sat down at our table. Taken aback, I pulled away from my mistress's embrace. Startled, she stared at the interloper.

"Young man, can you not see you are disturbing us?"

I was struck dumb. Entirely unflustered, he leaned towards her and, looking straight into her eyes, seized the hand that had, only moments before, been clasped in mine, and held it to his lips.

"We have not had the honour of being introduced. I am one of your most fervent admirers. I was dazzled by your flawless performance as Annette in *Les Amants terribles*, and by the depth of your portrayal of Medea, that devourer of children."

There was a beat of silence that only added to the drama, then he spoke again, dealing the killer blow. I sat and watched the vertiginous spectacle of my son stealing my lover in front of my very eyes, as he emulated the virile, brazen confidence of his idol Jean Gabin.

"I would take their place only too gladly."

At last he let go of her hand. He was only sixteen, but he was acting as though he were twenty-five, and his physique must have pleased Clotilde, as I couldn't help but notice.

With this, Guillaume got up and left, without a glance in my direction, thus making clear what was already quite obvious: in the blink of an eye I had become simply insignificant. Clotilde could not hide her confusion and, what was worse, seemed not to care.

There was nothing I could say to sidestep my humiliation.

"Well. Goodness me. Ah, allow me to, er, introduce my son."

She opened her eyes very wide, completely caught off guard, then burst into the heartiest laugh I have ever heard. Between gasps of mirth, she said:

"Well, well, well. Your succession is guaranteed."

With tears in her eyes and doubled over with mirth, she eventually regained her composure. In the gleam of desire that lit up her eyes I already knew that my son and this young woman would not be kind to me.

Loubna, 2005

Almost every single one of the letters from this remarkable assortment of women recounted a callous, wounding separation, and confirmed a dramatic change in my grandfather's manner. This man, who had up until then been so affectionate, so attentive with embraces and promises for the future, had suddenly become a bastard. His lovers, who seemed to come from every social class and were of many different nationalities, seemed no less surprised than I was, reading about their rejection. I began to skim rapidly through the letters. Even though somewhere among them I might find the nub of the situation, I had the feeling I wasn't going to find the real clue as to what had pushed my grandfather to betray his country – if that is in fact what he had done – simply because none of these women would have expressed such surprise if he'd confided in them. Their letters told me nothing more than what he wanted to be known, whether consciously or not. None of them would reveal where the money had come from – a gigantic sum for the time – that my grandmother had received from my grandfather, nor would they tell me how she had found herself the owner of an entire apartment building.

I thought back to the documents I'd read first, the top-secret statements made by witnesses to the explosion, which I'd found in the envelope Anis had given me. They described an initial detonation on the stern that would have killed several sailors – but not all. Some men, those with the fastest reactions, had managed to dive overboard. A second explosion, soon after the first and a great deal more powerful, managed to completely destroy part of a nearby building, which was reduced to a heap of rubble. Witnesses watched, powerless to help, as the men trying to swim away from the ship were knocked unconscious by huge slabs of sheet metal and jagged hunks of steel, before disappearing beneath the waves. They didn't survive the shock.

Fatimah was chuckling to herself as she read the sentimental prose that I'd put aside for the moment.

"What a charmer he was! I'd like to have known him. He clearly wasn't just any old bloke. They fell at his feet, one after the other."

She looked at me with utmost seriousness.

"I have to admit I get it, when you see him in uniform."

She handed me a black and white photograph inside an envelope made of a sheet of folded paper. It showed Guillaume Straub standing between a couple of much shorter sailors, one arm resting on each man's shoulders. He was a good two heads taller than them both. His smile looked strangely familiar.

"Do you think I look like him?"

She took the photograph from my hand. On the back was written *"Casablanca, 1939"* in a neat, sloping hand – just a few months before his death. Perhaps my father had already been conceived by then. Was the smile on his face that of a man happy he was going to be a father, or did he not know it yet? Or was he trying to find a way to extricate himself from a relationship he felt trapped in? Fatimah interrupted my train of thought.

"Well I'd say yes. Look how tall he is. You're the tallest girl I know. And then there's the way your eyes light up when you smile when you've got the sun in your eyes."

I batted her words away with my hand.

"Perhaps I'm just the result of a paid encounter between a French sailor and a prostitute from Bousbir."

She smiled. I think she was honestly trying to imagine herself in my place. Such an eventuality wouldn't have bothered her, but she knew me well enough to know I wouldn't be very happy about it. All my friends are very progressive, Fatimah most of all. They'd never dream of putting on a headscarf, in a country where it was an ancestral religious custom for a woman to conceal her charms.

"It's written in the Koran that women must veil their faces in order not to entice men other than their husbands. But there's a huge difference between not enticing and concealing! There's a huge difference encapsulated in the way translation has deformed the meaning. And don't anyone try to tell me it's got anything to do with fidelity. That's got nothing to do with the hijab," Fatimah often declares furiously.

I grew up with a group of close friends, both male and female, who talk freely about this, and have strong opinions on the subject. Among them are a psychologist and a singer, married respectively to a musician and a painter. All are members of the same sports club; they whizz around Casablanca on skateboards and take any opportunity to sunbathe in their bathing suits on the beaches along the Corniche.

Peering at the photo, Fatimah abruptly changed the subject. "Do you recognize this?"

She pointed to a concrete landing stage in the background of the picture.

"That's where the commercial port is now."

We used to play there all the time as kids, slithering on fish guts, racing between stalls loaded with bream, crabs and prawns left out in the sun; the stench was terrible. Just thinking about it makes my stomach turn.

Fatimah burst out laughing. "We were a lot less bothered by hygiene then than we are now. We didn't give a toss if we smelled of rotting fish!"

My grandmother Zayna used to love taking me there. I think she too would have liked to know my secret, to lighten the mysterious load I'd been carrying since I was born.

Fatimah looked at me and read my thoughts.

"You do have the same expression. Look at his smile: his eyes are creased and his cheekbones are high and wide, but even so he looks terribly serious. So much so it's impossible to tell if he's happy or deeply worried. You have that look some-times."

She went into the kitchen to make coffee and put out the pastries we'd bought from Madame Fhal before we came back to my apartment. We were enjoying our favourite, a walnut *fkass*, when all of a sudden, as I was leafing through the documents, my attention was drawn to a few in particular. They were also love letters, but had been filed separately from the others. They were marked with thick pencil strokes – there were question marks in the margin alongside certain sentences that had clearly puzzled the military censor. I read these lines attentively, trying to understand what it was that stood out about them more than in the other letters.

All were written in the same hand, and began in the same way, and what was most immediately striking about the content was that although there was obviously mutual affection and feelings of tenderness, the writer's passion for my grandfather was clearly not reciprocated. The writer seemed to be reproaching my grandfather for his growing lack of attention, but without in any way demonstrating the same animosity expressed by the other women he had dropped. The letters had been written over a longer period than the others; they seemed to have known each other for a long time and their correspondence ended only on the eve of the explosion. As the fatal date approached, the letters began to be covered in more and more red ink, furious crossings-out. The blue identified what was comprehensible, recurring, factual. And the red indicated something that appeared to have puzzled the reader.

21 March 1940
Casablanca

Guillaume, I haven't been able to stop thinking about you since the last night we spent together. I'm so desperate to be with you, to see other places, where we will wander and live what cannot be expressed openly.

The last line had been underlined furiously. Basically, in this romantic prose there was some kind of gap, or ellipsis, that was clearly only understood by the lovers.

I remembered what Anis had told me: the reason the letters had been preserved was because the French navy had doubted my grandfather's loyalty. In some of the earlier letters I'd read warnings from some of his other lovers, who were less strategic and probably mistrustful.

I'll always keep silent about the memories that sometimes overwhelm me at night. I would die of shame if anyone other than you were to read them.

In times of war soldiers are forbidden to reveal the locations where they have been posted, as well as what their missions are. They're kept under close surveillance. I wonder how many banal romances and declarations of love were read by the pen-pushers whose job was to protect military secrets.

I continued reading.

My husband hasn't confided in me for a long time. We are moving to New York. He has managed to get a transfer there.

I love you. What can I say; I prefer my lovers alive . . . I'm afraid for you. You're all I have.

Something struck me when I read this sentence. Something was staring me in the face. From her slightly affected style of writing it was obvious this woman had both money and education. But every one of her letters contained something slightly tongue in cheek, or a bit of slang that didn't sound quite right. She often ended her letters with an unexpected image or idiom.

That must have been what had drawn the attention of the censor, but apparently, considering the sheer number of question marks in the margins, he had failed to solve the riddle.

One of the letters had even been stamped by an official. Clearly it contained a sentence that had convinced the soldier to show it to an officer.

You know that a swimmer, as far as I'm concerned, is already a drowned man.

When you know what happened to the sailors on board *La Railleuse*, you can understand why that might have raised a few eyebrows. And then there was the fact that the woman, clearly wanting to conceal her identity, always signed her letters simply with the letter C, which must have been her initial.

Lucien, 1940

For weeks, my son did his best to steal my beautiful Clotilde away from me. And eventually he succeeded. Of course he did. That first meeting had been so very auspicious. What could I have done to stop him?

In the weeks that followed the encounter she agreed to meet me from time to time, but this was simply a tactic to reel him in. She knew he was trying to tear us apart, and had tacitly signed a macabre contract. For months, Guillaume had been effortlessly charming the same women I had seduced with considerable effort. My list of conquests was shrinking at a rate of knots – he was picking them off one after the other with cool determination. It was putting me increasingly on edge, while he appeared to be thriving more and more with every day that passed. He seemed to be enjoying deliberately re-minding me of my imminent decline.

"I'm afraid, Papa, it's all over for you, the chase," he'd say to me mysteriously. Each time he attacked my pride with even more enthusiasm, the issue for me being how to determine which of the women had betrayed me.

It was most painful when it came to Clotilde. It was a delightful diversion for her, and she was entranced to witness father and son fighting over her.

It was clear to me that while she had fallen more deeply in love with my son than any of the others had, he was using her to quench his thirst for revenge in this absurd contest.

Soon she was no longer paying me the slightest attention. Fundamentally, I was less afraid of losing her than of her telling him the secret that bound the two of us together. I knew I

wouldn't be able to stop her because, although it was unconscious, she resented me – for the weakness, fear and cowardice for
which she had never forgiven me. I saw the trap closing over
me, inexorable and pitiless. She told him everything.

That was when the blackmail began. He could no longer
bear to see me; he could not stand the sight of me. I wouldn't
wish on any father the pain I felt when I saw that I was nothing
but a spineless coward to him now. Until then the game he'd
been playing at least proved that I existed for him, that I was
sufficiently important for him to keep raising the bar. But now
his loathing for me was merciless.

He had me with this shameful secret. I couldn't risk losing
everything I'd built up. My family, my life after the war.

It had been so painful for so long. Flowers that had survived
long periods of drought were blooming now in the ravaged
earth. I had committed a shameful act, but I had been paying
the price of silence for many years.

My son and my mistress shared a mutual hatred for me. I
was lost. Guillaume gave me no alternative other than to sign
the authorization that would allow him to enlist in the navy. It
was a choice between him leaving or revealing the truth. And
this time I knew he might do it. I had ruined the life of this
woman I loved, and he was determined to make me pay.

A few years earlier she had fallen pregnant with my child.
She was desperate for this baby, since she and her husband
had been unable to have one together. I couldn't take the risk.
I was terrified, and I begged her to get rid of it. She wept,
argued, tried to persuade me. But I refused to give in. I had
my family, she had hers, and that was that. I couldn't conceive
of things any other way.

This was the reason Guillaume would not forgive me. I
might have had another family. He knew that with each love
affair I had, I came close to forsaking my own family and
establishing elsewhere what he believed was unique to us. And
yet I had refused to allow Clotilde to have a child with a secret
father, precisely because I was afraid that it would destroy my

family, that Hélène would leave me or hold me in contempt forever after.

So I capitulated. I signed.

When war broke out a few months later, I bitterly regretted my decision. It would have been better to break up my family than to sacrifice my son.

I remember that I sent him a note containing these few words of hope, forgiveness and love, in spite of his loathing for me: "You're just like me, your nickname is the Comeback Kid."

Felix, 1940

I left Maurice and Marcel. I couldn't bear to listen to them
spewing such awful things about Guillaume . . . I needed to
walk, to think and to sort through all the allegations they were
trying to stuff my head with.

I thought again about the woman in the djellaba who was
always hanging around the port. It's not like it was girls that
Guillaume was lacking. But I need to find her. And the more
I look back, the more things I remember.

There was one evening in particular . . . I don't know why,
but I'd bet my last penny that it was her. When there's nothing
to be suspicious of, it's the kind of detail you don't really think
much about . . . but when a scandal erupts, all of a sudden it's
the most important thing in the world, the only thing that
matters.

It was a few weeks before the explosion, maybe three, four
tops. We were propping up the bar in our favourite hangout
in Casablanca, three sheets to the wind already. It was shaping
up to be a fine evening. He liked a night out on the razzle, did
old Guillaume. He was a man of the world, and he knew how
to have a laugh, though it's true it had been a bit of an effort
to put a smile on his face the past little while.

As it happens, that evening he was as gloomy as a field in
the Somme region on a rainy November morning. He was
pretty depressing to be around. But that's not what made me
raise an eyebrow. No, what struck me was the woman. I hadn't
spotted her at first. Like I said, the evening was going pretty
well, and course I'm no head doctor, as I expect you've worked
out by now. At one point there we were, singing along to a

song by Fréhel, and out of the corner of my eye I saw him get up and saunter over to this bird. We ribbed him a bit, pretending that the song was about them. We were belting it out, not quite in tune, but it wasn't as if we gave a damn:

> *It's the blue java,*
> *The beautiful blue java,*
> *We're in a trance*
> *Face to face we dance,*
> *With a joyful rhythm,*
> *Our bodies are one.*
> *There's only one of her,*
> *It's the blue java.*

We kept winking at him, making saucy faces.

But instead of finding it funny, he ignored us. Actually, he turned pale, which made me laugh. I remember thinking, "I bet I know who's going to be the first to throw up tonight!" but when the song ended, I turned my head and saw that he'd sat down at the table behind us with the woman.

She was wearing a hijab and eyeing him intently. Good Lord! I couldn't say what was behind that intense stare, but it was as though her eyes were ablaze. I remember they were very bright, blue or green, I can't quite remember, and glaring daggers.

I don't think many people apart from me spotted what was going on; most of us were barely able to stand by then. He tried to take her hand. I remember being astonished to see this woman in a place like that, behaving the way she was.

Something didn't make sense. The tarts we knew would never get decked up like that. And the Moroccan girls who wore traditional dress weren't the type to be soliciting a sailor in some shoddy dive heaving with drunks.

Out of nowhere, she suddenly raised her voice in fury:

"You have to do it, Guillaume." Even Marcel heard that. He tried to turn round to look but he was swaying dangerously and lost his balance. He ended up flat on his back on the table behind us.

While we were cackling, Guillaume was looking downright uncomfortable. He was staring at his feet, ignoring everyone else. She sat down again, took his hand and held it to her cheek.

What could she have been up to? The thing that made it all so complicated was that in wartime it didn't take much to imagine she was some kind of Mata Hari. We knew perfectly well there were recruiters out there, and that they operated after dark, in bars. Thinking about it now, I have to admit that the officers' version, that he was a spy and a traitor, definitely makes the most sense.

But there's no way I could tell that to his family, to Lili.

I remember once after he'd been on leave in northern France, he told me how much cheese and wine he'd enjoyed; how he couldn't wait to go back.

It had all been a pack of lies. When his mother told me they hadn't seen him in more than a year, I managed to keep my mouth shut – but only just. I was squirming in my chair. I really didn't want to start suspecting my friend, that was the thing. Because that would've meant I'd been had, like a complete fool. His best mate. When you're fighting a war, lack of trust, it's like the worst thing of all. If you can't trust your mates – well, sooner or later you're buggered, aren't you?

I've got Lili's new address in Clermont-Ferrand, and I've promised her I'll go down and see her as soon as I can. There's other stuff, which I can't write down. Not least because I don't want to face the firing squad if they think I held my tongue. And then I've got to watch out for any ideas I might put into his family's heads. They couldn't deal with another terrible shock, especially his mother.

In her last letter, Lili told me she'd spent the week bawling her eyes out. It broke my heart. It was like her brother had snuffed it a second time. She got a letter from Ginette who told her she'd run off with Étienne and she never wanted to hear another word about that bastard Guillaume, dead or alive.

Lili must have told her parents to let go of any hopes they still had. She didn't tell me how that conversation had gone; I don't know how she'd have found the words to describe it. But silence encourages the imagination.

She told me she was dying to see me even more, that she dreamed of seeing me burst into the courtyard like last time, and she couldn't wait to throw herself into my arms.

"But I'm begging you, please don't come in uniform this time. My mother really couldn't cope with that."

Hélène, 1940

It's true I was rattled by the letter, but the main thing is that it made me realize I've never really believed my son is dead. The more I think about it the more convinced I am: Guillaume's not dead. I would know it in my guts if he had been killed. I reread all his letters looking for the names of all his navy friends, as well as those he had gone to see when he was on leave from Marseille, Toulon, Bizerte, Dakar, and of course Casablanca. I'm determined to find out what happened to him. There must be some kind of a clue, some tiny detail, in his letters. He learned how to write back to front so that the words can only be deciphered in a mirror, but everyone in the navy knows that trick. And he always had a taste for riddles and codes – he must have devised one. If he has deserted, he'll find a way of letting us know.

The one thing I'm desperate for is a ceasefire, even right in the middle of the fighting, so we can go home. If he's alive, I know he will have sent us a sign. There might be a letter on the kitchen table, or a book left out for us to flick through . . . There has to be some kind of message for us.

Meanwhile, Lili is blossoming. She never stops thinking about her brother, of course, but she is growing prettier every day. Meeting Felix has changed her life, I can see it only too clearly. I am envious of how carefree she seems, of this love affair that for the time being holds so much promise. Felix writes to her regularly, as often as his limited free time and the postal service allow. He has told her there have been some new developments. They'll be seeing each other soon and he will explain everything. He has been making inquiries, but he will explain it all in person. That is the proper way to do things, he says.

We all know that these words don't entirely reflect the reality of the situation. He isn't so much trying to respect convention as to avoid crystallizing any suspicions anyone might have about him. Bearing in mind what he has found out, he must be afraid of being thought complicit in Guillaume's desertion. And so, for different reasons, we are all waiting for his arrival with great impatience.

I am trying to kill time by doing what I know how to do: making clothes. Gradually, I have built up a modest clientele. Word has got round that I'm reliable, and can get hold of pretty fabrics. Even with rationing, I am keeping alive the memory of better times, when women still permitted themselves to make an effort with their appearance. Even though practical styles are called for now, because all the women I'm dressing need dresses and pinafores that are comfortable and they can work in, I always add a little detail to distract from the prevailing gloom: a sweetheart neckline to emphasize a shapely bosom, or a gently fitted waistline, even if the figure is bowed by despondency. But most important of all, I am fast. Since the war broke out, I have barely been sleeping, and needlework is a way of warding off insanity. I set up my studio in a corner of the attic where we have been living for the last few weeks. At 4 a.m., at the first glimmer of daylight, I throw myself into stitching up a hem or tacking together two pieces of fabric. I only use the sewing machine after Lucien and Lili have got up, at around 7 a.m. After a quick breakfast I have the attic to myself for the rest of the day, and I shut myself inside. At first my daughter or my husband used to pop in to say hello from time to time, when they had a moment, but they soon stopped bothering. Greeted by silence, or irritated muttering, they soon learned to beat a retreat. I can't bear anyone to be around me and making conversation is more than I am capable of.

I want to curl up with my memories, bring Guillaume back as quickly as I can, and I imagine our reunion again and again.

I whisper to him, and, when I know the house is empty, I even talk to him out loud.

I trace his face in folds of fabric, as I cut, adjust and sew. I invent scenarios in which the outcome of the war shows that my son was right to have deserted: he did it for the most noble of causes that only time will reveal. Or I imagine finding him after the war is over, safe and sound in some faraway country, like in the film *Coral Reefs*, a swarm of children hanging off his legs.

Reality, with the news becoming ever more alarming, is unendurable, and the only way I can cope is by retreating into my fantasy world. I am careful not to tell a soul. Not for all the world will I share my Guillaume with anyone.

Liliane, 1940

Since the devastating blow of Ginette's letter, so filled with hatred, we were all simply trying to keep busy, and we spoke to each other as little as possible. Going to work was a genuine relief for me. We shared daily tasks and meals with Uncle François and Aunt Édith, who had no children of their own. The atmosphere was gloomy, like endlessly grey, rainy days.

The clink of cutlery on china made me shudder, to the point that I had to keep myself from screaming just to break the deafening silence.

My life revolved around letters from Felix. My heart beat wildly when one arrived, and I would write back immediately. I kept my mind on our correspondence, which allowed me to distance myself from my parents' gloom and the awful reality I now had to live with: my brother was dead.

As summer drew on, my father grew increasingly anxious. He was waiting for something, and it wasn't the end of the war.

I sometimes came across him writing long letters. Every so often he asked me to post some for him, while others he would slip into his jacket pocket, murmuring, "I'll post this one, it'll take my mind off things to take a walk into the village."

Looking at the addresses, I would see he had written to Parliament, to the parents of Guillaume's friends – some of whom had also been stuck in Casablanca and would have seen the accident take place – to the captain of *La Railleuse*, to the Admiralty, and to the mayor of Villers-Carbonnel.

He was desperate for news – of Guillaume, of his factory,

of our old life – to try and raise his spirits. Since the rows that had driven me from the house several months earlier, I hadn't seen my parents address a word to each other. My mother had settled into a dreadful silence that nothing seemed able to break. She sewed, and read and reread Guillaume's letters.

The last time I'd spoken to her was to tell her that Felix had news for us. Perhaps I should have kept it to myself, because it was harder for our broken hearts to hold on to hope, to remain in this state of limbo, than to be in actual mourning.

I was desperate to see Felix again and to begin our life together. I stopped pestering him with questions about Guillaume: I knew he couldn't answer them, and the frustration of not knowing had been chased away by the simple pleasure of receiving Felix's love letters, in which he kept casting back to our first and only kiss.

Today he sent me a cutting from a newspaper about the funeral of the victims of the explosion on board *La Railleuse*. It had taken place in Casablanca, at the Ben M'sik cemetery. There were photographs of officers standing on some steps, all lined up like dominoes. One of them was General Noguès.

I wanted to show the article to my father. I found him in the stable, and I realized, with a feeling of panic, that it was ages since I'd had a real conversation with my parents. It was as if the silence between us had become irreversible.

My father glanced at the text and lingered over the photographs, then looked at me in a way he never had before. It was as though he had realized I wasn't a little girl any more.

"I have to tell you, Lili, I have written to everyone. I didn't want to say anything, but I think you are old enough to know. I have done what no one else would have done, I have asked for your brother's body to be repatriated to France. Partly because if it turns out that he isn't dead, that will be evidence that we had no idea what he was up to. But also because if he is dead, I want proof. I have to see his body, to be absolutely sure."

I wonder if this fixation is shared by all those who have lost loved ones: a desire to repudiate the facts, to make the truth perjure itself, force it to recant.

He drew out of his jacket pocket some tattered, dog-eared letters. He must have been carrying them around for weeks, reading them in rare moments of solitude, trying to work out what they were telling him.

"There's a lot of mumbo-jumbo. They're sailors, after all – you can't ask too much of them," he said with a wry smile. "But when I read them closely, I get the feeling they're playing for time, making me negotiate a maze of administrative demands."

I sat down on a bale of hay and read the letters one by one, in chronological order, trying to understand what he was trying to do. He hovered by my side, waiting for me to finish reading. With the tip of a stick he etched patterns into the dust, then rubbed them out with his toe.

He had been trying to contact all the organizations that might be able to furnish him with official proof of my brother's death, and had also made an official request for a death certificate and the repatriation of the body, "so that we can plan a funeral, which will facilitate the process of grieving for a devastated family".

The first reply he received was from the captain of *La Railleuse*.

Dear sir,

I am replying without delay to your letter which I recently received. I understand only too well your sorrow, and indeed I share it. I hardly need tell you that we are living through a terrible time, and for this reason I am writing personally to the family of each of the tragically deceased members of my crew.

Your son was killed outright in the horrific explosion that destroyed half of the ship. He would have had no time to suffer, or even to realize what was happening, of this you may be certain. Unfortunately, his body has not been recovered. We did, however, have a ceremony for him at the Ben M'Sik cemetery, in Casablanca, on 30 March, where he was laid to rest with the other victims of the disaster. His grave is marked by a stone cross with his name chiselled on it. It will be planted with flowers and carefully maintained, and I will certainly make sure to visit it every time I pass through.

The captain outlined the procedures to follow to assert our material rights as the family of the fallen.

Guillaume Straub died in combat; our victory will be thanks to his sacrifice. Let this be a cause of sorrowful pride for his family.

The next letter was from a member of Parliament who, to my surprise, addressed my father as "My dear friend".

"In a former life, I moved in high society," revealed my father enigmatically.

The letter was full of friendly platitudes; the minister and my father appeared to have known each other well and to have developed a genuine friendship:

I was so happy to hear that your daughter is with you, safe and well.

I was discovering a whole area of my father's life that I'd had no idea about. Seeing my father in this new light, I felt a flood of affectionate warmth towards the man who had talked about me to these people I did not know.

Since resigning from the Somme Refugee Committee that I set up, I have had almost no news from the region. The government is working to set up a service for reuniting families, specifically to enable people to return home. I managed to locate the whereabouts of a comrade of your son from La

Railleuse, *another boy from the Somme region. He survived,*
as you may be aware. I enclose a letter from his father. Please
let me know if there is anything more I can do, as a token
of my regard and in memory of the good old days.

The letter, from the father of a young man named Lejeune,
was in the same envelope. His handwriting was less confident,
his tone more direct, and his news less upbeat.

Mr Straub,
  My son Pierre has been in Casablanca for the last couple
of months. In his most recent letter home, he told me that
the ship your poor son was on is still in the port. Divers are
taking it apart for scrap. Pierre will make it a priority to go
and visit your son's grave as soon as he is next on leave. I
expect he will tell me about it in his next letter. I understand
that your son's body has not been found, but those who
witnessed the explosion cannot imagine that anyone could
have escaped with his life. I will of course send you further
details as and when I receive them.

I laid the letter on my knee. The same questions and the
same suspicions kept coming back. No one has been able to
confirm that he is dead. Everyone simply concludes that he
couldn't possibly have survived the carnage.

My father took one last letter out of his pocket.

"And then there's this one."

It came from the prefecture of Casablanca, Kingdom of
Morocco, and was signed by the Governor of Casablanca
himself.

To Mr Lucien Straub,
  I have the honour of informing you that we have found
no proof of Mr Guillaume Straub's death. The Admiralty's
inquiry remains ongoing. We will, of course, keep you informed
of any developments.

I was beside myself. "What on earth does that mean?"

"You're looking at a demonstration of sheer bureaucratic incompetence. The different versions all contradict each other, because, in fact, no one knows anything at all. Some people clearly don't even know what they're allowed to admit they don't know."

He picked up the letters and carefully folded them before slipping them back into the inside pocket of his jacket, next to his heart.

"Having said that, they really don't seem to know any more than we do."

I felt heartened by the last letter, however. "But he's alive, Father. Don't you see? I'm sure of it. They're hopping mad in Casablanca, because he's got away and he was so much smarter than everybody else. That's a fact, and they're furious."

My father smiled sadly at me. I refused not to revel in this good news: it was yet more evidence that he hadn't died in the explosion. If there was no body, it was obvious he wasn't dead.

Lucien, 1940

I've been lending François a hand in the fields. It's harvest time already. Lili has been helping with the apple crop. It's hard for a girl who's never had to work. We brought her up in relative affluence; the business I built up meant I was able to provide for my family and ensure a comfortable future for them. That was all I thought about after I came back from the front. As the mud churned in the trenches after a shell exploded close by, I used to think: "Lucien, if you get out of here alive, you're going to work so hard to shield your family as much as is humanly possible from all the shit that life has in store. They'll never go hungry, and won't that be something – to live in peace, without fear of scarcity or cold?" I repeated it to myself so many times that I think in the end that's what saved my life. It took my mind off dying. I told myself that if I made it out alive, I'd work my fingers to the bone, work myself to death, all for the sake of my family. That would be a hell of a lot more useful than ending up as sausage meat in a puddle in Verdun.

And when I returned home, that's exactly what I did. Hélène had already given birth to Guillaume and it killed me to think that she had spent the war assembling ammunition ten hours a day in a factory where she froze in winter and boiled beneath the white-hot corrugated-iron roof in the summer. So I began beavering away and, with my soldier's pension and a year of putting aside the salary from my job clocking in at a textile factory thirty miles from home (I cycled there and back every day), I bought a modest plot of land behind our house and in 1920 set up the first textile factory in the Somme region. Lili was born the following year, and this time Hélène did not have to work all the way through her pregnancy.

It's hard to think of all my factory workers who also had to leave the area, and of the factory itself, which was thriving, doing better than anywhere else around. We were in the throes of expansion when war broke out and ruined everything, all our technical developments of recent years. That unforgettable day, in the early 1930s, when the foreman and I purchased our first automatic loom – I remember it like it was yesterday. It simplified the workers' task, made it less gruelling, and we all felt like we were taking part in the great march of progress. We invested in twenty of these machines, and the outlay soon paid for itself. It was a memorable, marvellous decade, and it seemed as if nothing could touch us. Guillaume and Lili had a secure place in this well-oiled world, just as I had dreamed during the Great War.

And then, in a fraction of a second, there we were with nothing left at all.

But these are just material concerns. I am a great deal more worried about Guillaume. I know only too well the fate reserved for deserters, and I am fairly sure he has deserted. Even as early as 1914, on the eastern front, the generals had lines of snipers behind the lines of attack, for those who had the bad idea of not wanting to die on the spot. We had the choice between a bullet in the belly or a bullet in the arse.

François and his wife say little in front of Hélène, who hasn't spoken a word since we arrived in the Auvergne. She has shut herself up in a state of contemplation that sometimes horrifies me. She seems more and more like a nun in a state of beatitude, but I know that grieving is a long and painful process, especially when one doesn't know whether or not the mourning is warranted.

I think François had been considering it all in a fairly detached way. Until today, when he exploded.

"Good God, Lucien, it's not possible, all the bad luck you've had. It makes me absolutely furious. You're capable, you've

taught yourself to do so many things, you're so far from lazy
. . . You had everything you needed to succeed, and it's all gone
to the dogs."

I did my best to put on a brave face, telling him I would go
back to my factory, my workers and my family as soon as the
war was over.

I'll never forget the look he gave me. He placed his hand on
my shoulder and I could see in his eyes that I was far from
understanding the situation.

"Bloody hell, Lucien, are you going to force me to tell you
a few hard truths? Your son is dead. And yes, the war will end
eventually, and it would be better for us if it were sooner rather
than later, but when you get back to your factory, you're going
to find a big sign over the door saying Kraut & Co!"

I haven't said a word about my son and our suspicions that
he might be a deserter or a traitor, but his words hit me hard.
Just because his corpse hasn't been found it doesn't mean he
isn't dead, yet for weeks now I've stopped believing that he is.
But how often did I see on the battlefield how they gave up
trying to gather all the body parts. I have sent some letters and
received information from various people, as well as his personal effects, but none of this proves anything. As for the factory,
I know only too well that François is right. I have to be prepared for the worst. After all, we didn't even see it coming.

I was gathering my thoughts in reply when he threw another
punch.

"I have no idea how to tell you this, or how serious it could
be. After all, we have never experienced what you're going
through, this . . . disaster. But I think you should know: Hélène,
she . . . she spends all day talking to herself. I think she needs
something to distract her. She should come downstairs, don't
you think?"

"But she's reading and making clothes up there. She's keeping
her head and her hands busy in the way she knows best. It's
true she doesn't want to leave the attic, it's the shock; but she'll
get over it. She's very strong."

I have stopped trying to understand why Hélène has chosen this way to pass the time and keep her dark thoughts at bay. I have seen her reading and rereading Guillaume's letters. During the first months after he left, in 1936, when he'd just begun his basic training and it was still impossible to imagine there was going to be another war, he taught himself to write entire letters in mirror writing. We ended up learning this trick ourselves, to pass the time. Well, would you believe it, the other day I found Hélène peering at the letters through a magnifying glass, underlining words and muttering something I couldn't make out. She was deeply preoccupied and I was unable to distract her. She seemed to be trying to trick herself out of her worst fears. I think she was trying to work out when the fear of death had begun to fill the head of her darling boy, if he had been suffering during his final months, or if he had lied to us and betrayed himself. I suppose she was searching for a clue that would point to the change of mood Felix had described to us, but she said nothing. I left her to choose the right moment to open up to me.

François bowed his head and sniffed discreetly, then straightened up. It seemed he had more to tell me.

"She gave Édith a pile of dresses to deliver to her clients."

He stopped again. I was growing quite impatient. I wasn't used to discussing my private affairs and I didn't understand what he was getting at.

"Yes, good. So?"

"Well, the thing is – there are no clients, Lucien! Think about it! Who can afford to buy new clothes any more?"

Liliane, 1940

I didn't give my father time to react. I leapt up and left the room, calling back to him: "I'm going to show this to Mother! She can't refuse to believe the Governor of Casablanca himself."

I was already bounding up the stairs to the attic two at a time.

"Mother, good news, read this!" It was so dark that for a few moments I couldn't make out her hunched figure at the back of the room. She was sitting behind a sheet that she had hung up. She hadn't needed to ask us to respect the privacy of the little corner that she had fitted out. With an unspoken understanding, neither Father nor I had tried, or even thought of trying, to cross the line demarcated by the shabby, greying piece of fabric.

But this news was too good not to share. She had to know. I was even secretly hoping it might cheer her up a little, and she might agree to allow a little daylight in.

I gently pushed the sheet aside.

"Look, Mother, you have to read this . . ."

I stopped, stunned at the dreadful sight of the thing that she had been working on for weeks. The back wall was entirely papered with my brother's letters, from floor to ceiling, all meticulously annotated in red. I looked at my mother, who still hadn't deigned to raise her head. She was sitting at the table examining a sheet of paper with a magnifying glass, a pencil in her hand.

"Put it here, please," she said, pointing to a corner of the desk. "It's another letter from your brother, I suppose. I'm just correcting the others. I'll give him his lesson a little later on. Will you look at this dictation! It's full of mistakes. He's going to get an earful later, believe you me."

IV

True Love Lasts Forever

Clotilde, 1940

Lucien's wife, Hélène, had long known he was unfaithful to her. He and I had been together for years before I met her. It was 1935, before my first encounter with Guillaume.

I was standing in front of the Théâtre des Ambassadeurs where we were performing in Jean Anouilh's *Y avait un prisonnier*. We had just finished the dress rehearsal, before the first performance that same evening. There was Hélène, waiting outside in the rain, tall and dignified. She looked as though she had been standing there for a long time and was prepared to wait as long as she had to. Lucien had shown me her picture and, apparently, she recognized me too. I didn't pretend to be surprised. I owed her that at least.

We went to the nearest café, the same one where, a few months later, I met Guillaume.

I had just ordered two glasses of champagne when she began her attack.

"Some women are mere playthings, others are more dangerous . . . I beg you, I made it through the war to start a family with him. You know him as well as I do – he's not going to give up his family. I can accept you seeing each other, but please, do me the favour of not trying to persuade him to abandon his family. I'm convinced that it would be for the best, for him as well as for you and for my children, if you didn't, how shall I put it, increase the chances of drawing attention to what's going on."

I used to be one of those lucky people who had never known what it was to suffer. Life had been generous to me, both in terms of intellectual and emotional gifts – and, thanks to my husband, material gifts too. He was an extremely wealthy man, and he plied me with dresses, jewellery and trips abroad. The only thing he had not been able to give me was a child. That was when I had begun to suffer. Until I met Lucien. How cruel it was to discover how meaningless a life can be that had hitherto been cloudless, but now would never see the sun.

I remember Hélène as a very dignified woman. In spite of the disaster that had befallen France, I had beautiful jewellery and clothes; yet I felt wrong somehow, envious of what she had.

I never found out how or thanks to whom she found out about my pregnancy, or if it was an instinct as sharp as that of a wounded animal who scents danger all around. But she knew.

Now we were both in possession of this secret. She looked down at my stomach. I was still able to hide the pregnancy beneath my loose-fitting coats and I wore eye-catching necklaces to distract attention from the rest of my body.

"What are you going to do?" she asked.

There was not an ounce of animosity in her voice. Not the faintest trace of bitterness. Just a profound fear that she managed to control, while remaining utterly sombre. That was the moment I made the decision. It wasn't anything to do with Lucien's refusal. Seeing him so afraid, backing away from his responsibilities, had almost been enough to convince me to keep the child despite his opposition. But with her it was different. I could not understand what had led her to accept her husband's infidelities all these years.

"I made a commitment to him and I cannot imagine loving another man. I know you have a version of him, but let's agree it's of little consequence. I know how seductive he can be when he puts his mind to it. But you don't know him like I know him. I'm sure he never tells you his nightmares, does he? I'm sure he doesn't show you his dark side. Am I right?"

"No, he doesn't."

When he was with me he was nothing but charismatic, masculine charm.

"You are part of and you represent a world he secretly aspires to; but he will never completely belong to you, because he knows that with you, he can never reveal his despair."

She looked me up and down. Not so much with envy as with curiosity.

"Looking at you, I don't get the feeling that you're the kind of woman who would support a man – in the sense of propping him up, being his rock. Lucien gets the strength that makes him so desirable from me. Without his family, without me, he would collapse like a house of cards. And if – to answer the question that you've surely asked yourself – I accept all this, it's because he was, and in my eyes still is, a good man. He loves us, our children and me, with a devotion that has withstood everything."

And then she delivered the final blow.

"You'll tire of this relationship. And I think he knows it."

Secretly I had always known.

The next day I visited a backstreet abortionist in Tannerie Street, in Belleville, far from the areas of Paris I normally frequent. In a place and a situation like this, all women are equal. Rich or poor, we all end up in agony lying on the kitchen table in a small apartment, choking on the fumes from a gas stove in the corner with its persistent, insipid smell of vegetable soup, the long needle planting itself in our flesh, as we pray we will survive.

The pain was awful the next day, and it grew worse. Something was wrong. My womb had been perforated, and I learned that I had aborted the only child I would ever carry. Once upon a time I had wandered in a silken negligee around my apartment with its view onto the Eiffel Tower. I had worn satin evening gowns on stage. Now I had been rendered infertile on a checked tablecloth that smelled of onions.

Loubna, 2005

Wear something nice.

My date with Ali was approaching. He was coming to pick me up in a few hours' time and I still had no idea what I was going to wear. I called Liz in desperation and she told me to come over to her apartment. She had some dresses she could lend me and was tickled pink to hear that Ali and I were seeing each other again. I suspected she wanted to grill me about what had happened after our nocturnal visit to the house.

She assured me her clothes would fit; we were almost the same size. I was maybe a bit slimmer than her, and she was a little taller than me. I took with me a pair of black stilettos and some brown leather high-heeled sandals. Depending on the outfit, one or other would suit.

I found a taxi almost straight away. The driver wanted to chat – he was in a cheerful mood because he was about to become a grandfather – and he spent the journey kissing his hand and lifting it to the sky to thank God for the gift He was giving him.

I couldn't concentrate on what he was saying and simply nodded and smiled politely. My mind was wandering all over the place; I couldn't stop thinking about all those sentences circled in red. They were so familiar. It felt like I had the words on the tip of my tongue. It was as though I could grasp their contours for a moment, like I was on the verge of understanding, but every time, at the last moment, my memory failed me. I slapped my thigh in frustration after yet another aborted attempt to work it out, and the driver turned round to look at me. We'd arrived. He dropped me at Rick's Café. I got out of the car and while I was paying him, congratulated him on his soon-to-be-born grandson: "May God protect him!"

The restaurant was closed, and suffused with an atmosphere of controlled agitation. Everyone was busy; it was like a waltz that they all knew by heart. Everyone had their job in this shadowy environment, which let no light in from outside.

"It's so much more romantic and seductive when you don't know if it's daytime outside or not. Like in those places where people play poker. Daylight makes people sensible, darkness gives them permission to be distracted," Liz once said to me.

We met in her apartment above the café. She was really happy to see me, and her curiosity was at fever pitch, as I'd guessed it would be. She bombarded me with questions before she got out the different outfits she'd told me about.

"Liz, I have nothing juicy to tell you. I don't know if he's decided to invest in my project. He didn't say anything last time. The evening ended rather abruptly."

I tried on the first dress. It was short, black, plain, backless and figure-hugging, with a lace detail at the shoulder. My stilettos would go perfectly. I showed her the result and, without waiting for her to comment, told her the last words that Ali had said to me and about the forty-eight hours that had followed.

She held out a second, absolutely stunning dress, with a bead- and sequin-encrusted bustier and ribbons of topstitched embroidery. It was cut close to the waist, before flaring out at the hips in a cloud of tulle.

"You didn't think I was going to let you go out to eat with one of the richest men in Morocco in any old dress, did you? Elie Saab. One of the reasons I regret not moving to Beirut."

I tried it on. It was perfect. Obviously.

"Just what you need to make him regret his lack of manners," Liz said.

I slipped on my stilettos and glanced in the mirror. I looked beautiful. The dress looked good on me, and it would look good in his Maserati too.

Nevertheless, I was nervous about our impending rendez-vous. Ali made me feel uncomfortable, and the things I'd discovered over the last couple of days had unsettled me more than I'd realized. Standing there in front of Liz made me realize the extent to which these women's letters had revived an old bitterness in me. About my father, that he'd died when I was so young, leaving me nothing but a few memories. About my grandfather, whom I'd idealized as a war hero until today. I'd been cloistered in a fantasy of my father and grandfather as saviour figures who had signed up to a noble cause and died for their ideals. No man could match them in my eyes. I hadn't had time to dissect this fantasy in order to be free of it.

I'd been brought up by two single women, my mother and my grandmother, detached from two men whose absence weighed heavily. Strong, independent women, they had brought me up with an iron hand, an orchid in an urban jungle. They had taught me to respect my body and love myself for who I was.

Women can deal with anything, Loubna.

And of that, I was deeply convinced. I had been raised with the idea that women are strengthened by their independence, and only a few, rare, special men are worthy of them. When my father died, my mother swore that she would never live with another man, "unless he was as wonderful as your father was".

I had never given too much thought to my family; knowing nothing about it had nourished a private mythology that I had immersed myself in from a young age. The truth that was now emerging could only damage the fantasy world I had created.

And my questions were coming thick and fast. Perhaps it was not by chance that my grandfather had behaved like such a Lothario with all those women? His change of mood, the way he had gone so quickly from affectionate to vile, with women who only wished him well – did all this conceal something more serious?

Liz served us each a cognac in those balloon glasses you cradle in your hand to swirl the golden liquid around so that its gorgeous aroma can bloom. She giggled. She'd kicked off her shoes and her legs were dangling over one arm of her club chair, her back leaning against the other, so she was facing me. In that pronounced New York accent that I suspected her of exaggerating whenever she talked about sex or American politics, she said, "Honey, stop being so uptight! And let me tell you, you're not in the right frame of mind for going to dinner with Ali. You always see things in black and white. With you, it's always one thing or the other. Life is about compromising, it's about the opportunities that you choose to take after a bit of negotiation – you need to learn the meaning of that word."

I sank down into the depths of my leather chair and breathed in the alcoholic vapours from my glass. I sipped it slowly, as if I was celebrating the last day of my former life. I was about to leave black and white behind, for all the other shades.

Clotilde, 1940

Until the abortion I had always been in full control of my life. Then everything began to unravel, with a terrible inevitability. A cruel irony turned this new despair into inspiration for my greatest role, far from the bright lights of the stage: the grieving lover of a young sailor.

Guillaume was barely more than a boy but, almost without realizing it, I was falling desperately in love with him. At the beginning we met behind his father's back, but very soon I gave up hiding it. We were both caught up in the game, until he left in late 1936. His tour of duty in the navy should have kept him far away from me, but I found this impossible to bear. I thought it would pass, that I would forget him. But we continued to write to each other, and I knew that when he had finished his training in Toulon he was to be sent to Casablanca. He was stringing us both along, Ginette and I. Although I was quite detached to begin with, very soon I was eaten up with jealousy at the thought of this girl who had the privilege of not even knowing that she shared her lover with other women.

My husband and I had a liberal marriage, and he knew all about my love for Guillaume. He was perfectly aware that there was simply no point in trying to punish me for it. He was sure that a relationship with a man so young was not a real threat. He told me almost daily that Guillaume would leave me.

"My dear, men are fickle, and never more so than when they're twenty. It's only age, and the fear of finding himself alone, that makes a man realize how fortunate he is to have a woman by his side."

I was inconsolable, and deaf to the rumblings of war intensifying in Europe. I even turned down the role of Valentine in Anouilh's *Le Voyageur sans bagage*.

My husband clearly believed I would get over it in time, but he was wrong. Frustration only made the relationship even more alluring. He agreed to leave Paris and his business interests, and proposed his services as deputy to the director of Shell in Casablanca.

In one sense, it was an excellent opportunity for him: he had been looking to sell his Parisian business, having been considering a return to London – which I was very much against. The febrile political situation was making business difficult; so much so that, in order to avoid a crisis in both his financial affairs and his marriage, we left for Casablanca at the end of 1937.

The crossing was blissful. The reunion with my lover even more so. Guillaume had matured and I found him more handsome than ever. I guessed he'd had some fleeting romances: he was different, less clumsy. But we shared so much more than that. Literature, cinema . . . we could talk about these things for hours on end.

He spent a great deal of time criss-crossing the Mediterranean in 1938, but he also spent lengthy periods in Casablanca, and his absences only made our passion more intense. Whenever he was on leave, I would pretend he was my husband's distant cousin, and we would go everywhere together: restaurants, cafés, casinos, yachts, private mansions. I introduced him to the smart set in Casablanca, people in the leading diplomatic circles, politicians and wealthy businessmen. 1938 was a wonderful year, awash with champagne and sunnier than I had dared imagine. When I think back to that time all I remember is sipping cherry liqueur on café terraces in the cool of the evening, our flirtatious conversations interrupted by musicians playing gypsy music in the humid streets around the port, dancing the tango at the open-air bars of Aïn Diab, playing poker in the casino on the Corniche, smoking cigars and sipping champagne. I don't know how he managed to bear returning to *La Railleuse*. What a shock it must have been, the contrast between the pleasures of the night and the duties of the day . . . But he never complained.

In reality, Guillaume was getting a taste for this life, and I suspect he would have left me sooner if I hadn't shared it with him. If the navy had been a childhood dream that he'd made the mistake of romanticizing, he realized that it was nonetheless a vital conduit that enabled him to discover a whole new world. He was counting the days until the end of his posting and the beginning of the new life he was plotting behind my back. But I did not discover this until much later. I was beginning to sense that my devotion to him was no longer reciprocal, but we were settled in our habits and I could not imagine the life we had ever coming to an end. Though he was as bored as I was besotted, I was quite unable to listen to reason.

My husband had his first ever fit of jealousy on New Year's Eve, 1939. That was the precise moment that everything changed. My husband was furious, my lover demonstrating nothing but the cruellest detachment, and I was in a turmoil of anguish.

My unfortunate husband had overheard some mocking remarks from his colleagues who – with the social world of the colonies being rather small and that of the colonialists even more so – were also our partners at the casino gaming tables, neighbouring diners at the Excelsior restaurant, fellow bathers at the swimming pool by the beach . . . In a nutshell, a rumour began to circulate about my undue affection for this "cousin" of ours.

"However affectionate one may be permitted to be in France, no one behaves like this with a member of their own family. People are not fools. They see you, they watch you. People with money have nothing better to do than scrutinize other people's habits and inappropriate behaviour. They may be pleasant to your face, but behind your back they're only interested in one thing, and that's to see you fall from grace. Everyone's talking about you, laughing about you, Clotilde, and I look like a fool."

Guillaume had become an increasingly important part of my life, and this was entirely my fault. I was no longer afraid of being seen in his company. The world of malingering French expatriates seemed so insubstantial to me, with all their absurd protocol and empty patriotic formalities. None of it was important, it seemed to me, or even real. I thought these people were all like me, just passing through, on this makeshift stage that they would abandon as soon as they had built up a decent fortune. I didn't give a damn about what they thought.

Only one thing concerned me, obsessed me in fact: the miserable spectacle of Guillaume's diminishing love for me, which was withering at the same rate as his interest in the smart set was growing. And when I say smart set, I really mean his interest in poker games and Salma, the daughter of a bourgeois Moroccan who had purchased a building on the Boulevard de France, a few metres from the Rialto and close to my own home.

Felix, 1940

I'd been looking into things since my visit to the hospital. So when I went back to see how the patients were doing, this time I was prepared, and I had a few questions.

Which meant that when they turned round and asked me why I was so interested in this stuff, I had my story ready: "Hey, come on, he was a mate of ours, wasn't he? Have you forgotten, Marcel, when those sharks nearly had you for dinner?"

The three of us, Marcel, Guillaume and I, had "crossed the line" – the equator – together. It's a tradition in the navy, an initiation rite, a baptism, for every sailor who crosses it for the first time. And when I say baptism, that's a fancy word to say you get dipped in the sea. We had to put on these ridiculous costumes, make funny speeches in front of everyone on board, and then – eldest first – we'd all get ducked. We were already three sheets to the wind, but off we trundled, ready to dive overboard, with Marcel offering to go first. It's not something you do every day. But Guillaume hoiked him back – he saw the sea was seething with ravenous sharks. Lucky for him. We had to make do with the swimming pool at someone's house later on.

"You have to give him credit for that, Marcel. He saved your life that day!"

"I'll give credit to the Moroccans who helped us. The ones who fished us out of the water, fed us and took care of us. The people who took in anyone who wasn't in too terrible a state, in order to take the pressure off the hospital."

Marcel had tears in his eyes, and I realized that accounting for all the victims hadn't been as precise that day as we'd been led to believe. Which made me think that if that was the case, Guillaume could be somewhere in Casablanca, completely oblivious, with no idea what his name was or what the hell he was doing there! That's the kind of thing that happens in wartime. I was told about a distant cousin of my father during the last war. It took them more than ten years to find him, and when they did it was purely by chance.

But the most interesting thing was what Marcel let slip. Apparently for weeks after the explosion, a beautiful woman, really classy, had been hanging around the port asking about Guillaume. My first thought was that she must be the one who'd been showing up every evening at the port alongside the gangplank of *La Railleuse*, all wrapped up in her djellaba.

"D'you have any idea how I could contact her? I think Guillaume's family is trying to find her, and she's trying to find them too. If there's anything I can do to help out . . ."

Even with his limbs all bandaged up and wounds that hurt like hell he was as dirty-minded as ever, and he gave me a sly little wink, filled with inuendo, and said how big-hearted I was, especially when it came to the pretty ladies.

"She was there most days. If you get a message to her, I expect she'll agree to meet you. She looked very anxious, too."

So I moved heaven and earth to find out how to contact her, and asked her to come to the harbour and wait for me – my name was Felix, and we had some mutual concerns. There weren't a lot of women hanging around there, and it wouldn't take me long to spot her.

It went according to plan – she was there the next day.

She was beautiful, very chic and elegant, just as the boys had described. I was a bit shy at first, but we had important things to talk about and I soon managed to stop thinking about her pretty eyes.

We went to a nearby café. It had a nice terrace, but she wanted to sit inside; she didn't want to be seen with me. Apparently she knew a lot of the French who lived in

Casablanca, some of whom had time to sit around in bistros in the middle of the afternoon, thank you very much. These were important people, you know!

I was growing more and more curious. I wondered what her relationship was with Guillaume.

We sat down at a table inside the Café de l'Empire on the Boulevard de la Gare, a beautiful art deco place. We each ordered a cherry liqueur. The waiter was better dressed than I was – but I didn't give a damn about any of that now that we were in the middle of a war.

I had a barrage of questions for her, as a result of knowing too much about Guillaume and at the same time not enough, and I decided to get straight to the point.

"Was it you who always used to be waiting for him at the port wearing a djellaba?"

She gave me a baleful look and didn't respond right away. Then she sat up straight and crossed one leg over the other. A flap of her skirt fell open, revealing her thigh, and I tried as hard as I could to focus on what she was saying because I was going to have to remember it later on.

"I was his lover. We knew each other for several years and were very much in love, though I more than he, I think."

Her voice held a hint of wry regret.

"It was indeed me, the woman you saw in a djellaba. I wanted him to come away with me. He always promised me he wouldn't end up getting killed. He often said so, and I wanted to help him keep his promise."

I looked at her. I thought back to all those moments, the weeks before the explosion, Guillaume leaning over the rails. I'd seen them exchanging furtive glances. I remembered her as well, in the bar that night, shouting out: "You have to do it."

She choked back a little sob, and added: "He said he would do it, if only for her."

"Who's 'her'?"

"He never told you about her? Ah. He must truly have been

in love if he kept her a secret. A Moroccan girl, your age or thereabouts. Salma was her name. In fact, I've been trying to find her. I was told that after the explosion she was wandering the streets around Ben M'sik like a lost soul. But I know perfectly well how it works here – all the things they're saying about Guillaume, everything they're trying to keep under wraps."

I'd heard it all too.

"So you don't know where he's gone? If he's left Casablanca? If he's still alive?"

"I have no idea. We exchanged a few letters. In code, I should add. I don't know what's become of him. All I know is he hasn't been found."

"Did you know he had shore leave that evening, but he offered it to me at the last minute?"

"No, I had no idea. In fact we were planning to meet that day. That's why I was waiting in the port by my car. We were supposed to be taking off. We were no longer lovers by then – we hadn't been for months – not since he'd met Salma, in fact. I was jealous, but that didn't mean I wanted him dead."

Her expression grew distant as she was swallowed up by memories, like quicksand.

"I met her at the military hospital. We were both looking for Guillaume. When I saw her, I understood they had planned to see each other again, that he had made promises to her. She was pregnant. She told me the only thing she cared about was finding Guillaume; she was about to give birth and they had been planning to escape together into the desert. I wanted to take her home with me, she was so pale. She must have walked a long way to get to the military hospital, in her state, in the heat. It can't have been good for her health. She promised she would come back the next day, but she had to pack. I gave her a large sum of money. I happened to have a lot on me that day: I had been planning to run off with Guillaume, so I was prepared."

That bitter little laugh again, the one that made her eyes disappear.

"She eventually accepted the money but she never came back. I don't know what happened to her. I've been trying to find her too – and him. Perhaps they're both in the desert by now, waiting for the madness to end? That's what I would have done in their place."

I saw her eyes fill with tears. She stood up. Just like that, she didn't want to say any more. That was it. But I still had some questions.

"The last thing he said to me was, 'I've got some things to sort out. I can't take leave right now.'"

Tears were rolling down her cheeks. She handed me a letter.

"I have his last words too; the last letter he wrote to me. It's for his family. I haven't heard from him since. It was the morning of the explosion. I still can't quite believe he's dead . . ."

She put a hand on my shoulder, looked at me with great tenderness, and got up to leave, putting a banknote on the table. She didn't wait for the change. As she left, she turned and added quickly: "Do you ever go to the cinema? I hope you know who Guillaume's favourite actor was. If you don't then you won't understand a thing."

Of course I knew. I watched her leave and it broke my heart because it was one of those moments that he'd have loved to see on screen. A beautiful, shapely woman weeping over him, then wandering off into the sunset. He wasn't even here any more, and he still managed to be the centre of attention.

His favourite films were *The Grand Illusion, Daybreak, Coral Reefs, Port of Shadows*. The hours he spent boring me to tears as he recited the scenes that had sent shivers down his spine . . . I sat there on my own nursing a cherry liqueur and thinking about him and all those scenes in black and white. The money she'd left on the table was enough for another drink, and then why not, one last one for the road.

Port of Shadows was an odd one. Guillaume identified even more than he usually did with the main character because he was a sailor trying to escape his fate, who all of a sudden found himself obliged to jump ship. There was something in it that got to all of us . . . When it gets under your skin like that, when it's so close to the bone, it can drive you mad.

When he talked about it there was this one thing that came up again and again, and each time it bothered me a little bit more. Whether it was in *The Human Beast*, *Daybreak* or *Pépé le Moko*, the Jean Gabin character always finds himself in an impossible situation that he can only get out of feet first. He's got a knack for keeping your hopes up right to the end, and then, no: it all goes wrong, in the worst way possible. Guillaume saw beauty there. He'd repeat Gabin's lines like he was hypnotized, and it scared the living daylights out of me. "It's when it's sad that it's beautiful, Felix. Don't you see that? He fights destiny because he wants to cut loose. Look at *Pépé le Moko* or *Port of Shadows*, the way he jumps ship because the navy's become a prison, it's stopping him from living the life he wants. It's the navy, but it could just as well be a contract, a doomed love affair, a boring life . . . The point is that you have to earn freedom, it has a price, but it's always worth trying your luck." Course, he made me feel like the biggest fool of all, because all I cared about was not seeing the inside of a prison, whatever that meant – according to him there was an infinite number of different kinds. I obviously didn't have his balls, because I'm just happy when life is straightforward and trouble-free.

"Another cherry liqueur, please! I don't want my memories fading on me!"

Loubna, 2005

Liz was right, of course. Everything's a compromise, between oneself and everybody else. I began to think about the man who might be about to invest in my project from this new perspective. I couldn't say yet what I would offer him in return.

I'd gone home to finish getting ready for my date with Ali, when Anis turned up. I chatted to him from inside the bathroom, from behind the closed door. I was putting on my makeup and it was so warm that I had taken off the dress in the bathroom, which was flooded with light.

"I can't stop thinking about the last lot of letters, the ones signed 'C'. There are whole sentences that sound like they're written in code, but the weirdest thing is that they speak to me, somehow. I mean – it's like I've heard them already."

I was so fired up that I didn't even wait for Anis to tell me why he'd come.

"Anyway, he was probably just like any other man. Uncomplicated. Not particularly demonstrative. I'm not sure my grandmother was any better. At worst, she was a prostitute who'd turned her best trick, and at best, a—"

I was putting on mascara. Anis interrupted me.

"You're so uptight, Loubna!"

There wasn't a trace of humour in his voice. He wanted his words to hurt me. I put on my dress as he continued talking.

"You know what I think is the biggest problem in the world? Being unable to talk about the female orgasm. Denying it even exists. Not understanding that what women want is exactly the same as what men want: to have the right to pleasure. To live their lives how they want. Our greatest tragedy is that we find it inappropriate that women orgasm like men, that they have the same desires. Your grandmother was in love with a sailor who made her come all night long! And maybe she didn't love him, but she did love how he made her feel. So what, Loubna? Good for her. At least she experienced it!"

His tone was growing heated. I heard what he was saying, and he wasn't wrong. I'd built a fortress around myself as defence against emotion. Of course, I would never intentionally hurt anyone, but I wouldn't be kind to them either. Anis carried on talking, without giving me a chance to respond. He obviously didn't even care what I thought. He was absolutely irate.

"I hate how bloody moralistic we all are these days. Do we need a war, the fear of dying, to make us dare to live a little?"

Warily, I came out of the bathroom in my beautiful Elie Saab dress. When he saw me, Anis stiffened. His deep voice gave way to heavy silence.

I'd never seen him like this, in a state somewhere between hatred and grief. His eyes were filled with tears of rage.

"Are you seeing Ali again? Really? After he had the nerve to say what he did about your family? About you, basically?"

"Yes, but . . . Why does it bother you so much?"

"He's an absolute bastard. Can you not see that? Everyone knows it. And the way he treats women, most of all."

He surveyed my dress, my hair, my makeup. He didn't recognize me. I could read it in his eyes.

"You women, you're worse than men sometimes. Constantly stabbing each other in the back, so you can win over some man who's got no principles or values. Moral values? What a joke! You couldn't care less about them. You want money and beauty, even though you don't want people to think of you that way. Think about it, Loubna. Why would you be ashamed of your grandmother? Because she was a prostitute? Who slept with a penniless sailor? For God's sake! Which one of you is selling herself now? Look at yourself! Anyway, you do have one thing in common with her: you think your life's a film, and you live it without the slightest concern for other people!"

He bent down and pulled out a list from his bag. The names of all the women who had given birth between 30 March and 5 April at the military hospital in Casablanca. There were only three. Which wasn't surprising, since the hospital had been built to treat soldiers, and there had been few women in the army at the time.

He left without another word. Three names: Édith Lejeune. Clarisse Emerson. Salma Akhbr. Three random names that anyone could have thought up. One of whom was my grandmother.

The list burned my fingers and Anis's voice echoed in my head. I had to be prepared to accept that Guillaume Straub and my grandmother might not have been in love. Why had it never occurred to me that my grandfather might not have been a hero; not, in fact, my ideal man personified?

Anis had never spoken to me like that before. I was completely stunned. And now he'd left me with this list of three names that was so important to me.

The first name I didn't recognize. Guillaume had had a friend called Lejeune, I'd seen letters from him, but nothing in them hinted at anything beyond their friendship, and it seemed like a common enough surname. I moved on to the second name. It particularly drew my attention because the most interesting letters were those signed C. She also mentioned a British husband, an industrialist. It was worth checking out, in any case. C for Clarisse, surname Emerson – that might correspond. The third name didn't mean anything to me.

When Ali turned up, he leaned over to open the passenger door and I was immediately struck by the way he looked at me. He hadn't been expecting to see me in a dress like this, and I couldn't help remembering what Anis had said. I still didn't know whether to be angry with him or beg his forgiveness. I remained silent as Ali drove us into town.

We were going to the Hyatt restaurant, near the United

Nations Square. We chatted about films and this time he didn't bring up my disreputable family origins. I was impatient to find out what he'd been thinking since we had seen each other last, and I tried to relax with the help of the wine.

I was agreeably surprised by the conversation, which was pleasant and flowed easily. If it hadn't been for the fact that he was potentially going to become my boss, this interview would have been the perfect first date – albeit slightly tarnished by Anis's disapproval. I remembered Liz's advice about negotiating and compromising. How stubborn was I prepared to be? For the time being, I decided not to think about it – a first compromise with myself.

The food was delicious, and Ali was charming and solicitous, as we discussed my passion, the cinema. Everything was perfect, like him. Like the previous time, when we'd driven to the tumbledown building at three in the morning.

I couldn't deduce anything from the easy atmosphere between us. I didn't know enough to guess what his next move would be, or if we were indeed playing a game. After dinner he invited me for a last drink in a bar on the Corniche. I imagined he was going to talk about my project. I sensed I shouldn't bring it up first – it wasn't for me to twist his arm – but the unspoken subject, insofar as it was there in the background, made me feel awkward. He appeared to find the situation amusing. He had created a warm atmosphere, a relationship of trust, that could come apart at the slightest false move. I knew that I was involved in a precarious balancing act.

He didn't talk on the drive to Corniche Boulevard, and he didn't look at me either, just like the other night. We walked into the bar and he chose the table furthest from the crowd, by the balcony. He'd reserved it. With barely a glance in my direction, he ordered two glasses of champagne.

"Let's talk business, Loubna. You know, I miss the days when you could risk everything at poker. When you could win or lose everything in the blink of an eye."

I didn't understand. I merely noted that he was addressing me with the familiar "*tu*".

He pulled a yellowing slip of paper from his pocket and continued, "Like the building you live in, for example." I unfolded the paper, which looked strangely familiar. Clearly, Ali was always going to be ahead of the game when it came to research.

"Apparently our families are linked by property."

I was holding a notarized agreement written in two hands that were completely unfamiliar to me: one was Jean Fanchon – "My grandfather," said Ali – and the other Guillaume Straub. It was a shock to see his signature. It was tangible proof that he had once lived and wasn't simply a figment of the imagination of all those young women.

"Your grandfather wanted the building for your grandmother to live in. She was pregnant, and her family had thrown her out because of their relationship. This was how he ensured that she would never want for money. Then, out of the blue, she disappeared. My grandfather did everything he could to try and find her. He used to say it was his worst memory. After it happened, he never played poker again."

Ali fell silent. Even if it hadn't been his intention, he had just restored the image that had been damaged by my reading my grandfather's correspondence over the last few days. Guillaume Straub had been a man who took his responsibilities seriously. My grandfather had not abandoned my grandmother for a life of frivolity. If he had deserted, it must have been for her, and something must have gone badly wrong. If he had been a traitor, it was because he had to get out, for her sake above all else.

Ali's voice broke into my thoughts.

"What about you? What risks would you take to have your cinema?"

His expression left me in no doubt as to what he was expecting from me. I suddenly realized the absurdity of the situation. In spite of Ali's success – the fact that he was a millionaire and a brilliant entrepreneur – he was still pained by the memory of his family's humiliation and felt compelled to try and avenge this ancestral grievance. He was obeying a law of revenge that had nothing to do with either of us. His eyes were filled with animosity.

I was suddenly relieved of the weight on my shoulders that he had made me carry. It was his secret that had been shackling me.

"I have nothing to give you because I have nothing to make amends for. There's no law of retribution that applies in this case! Look at this document: the building was won fair and square. If you and your family are bad losers, that's hardly my problem." He was stupefied, furious that history was repeating itself.

Ali had just set me free. With a deafening racket, all the barriers of misunderstanding finally came crashing down.

Clotilde, 1940

Guillaume had fallen in love at first sight. Everyone knew that Salma was the daughter of a bourgeois Moroccan man who had moved into a large mansion on the Boulevard de France. One Saturday evening, dancing at the lido in Aïn Diab, he suddenly stood stock still. He'd seen her. Salma Akhbr.

"You must introduce me. You know her, don't you? I saw you talking to her father at the theatre last week."

In spite of my determination to do nothing of the sort, I complied. Taken aback by the way that fate seemed determined to mortify me, I watched, powerless, exactly as Lucien had once stood by and watched as our love affair collapsed like a house of cards.

There was no doubt about their mutual attraction. Their love was simple and pure. Fated. There was absolutely nothing I could do to fight it. Even when her father threatened to disinherit her if she continued her infatuation with this "little sailor", declaring that he hadn't dragged his family into Casablanca's highest social circles for her to end up an ordinary commoner, wasting her time with underlings and nobodies. "I insist you give up my daughter. It's like feeding jam to a pig!" I heard him say to Guillaume one night, a few months before the explosion. There was fury in his voice, but Guillaume had no intention of giving an inch in the face of the promise the future now held for him.

Salma's father was furious. But all his entreaties, threats and invective came to nothing. The damage was done. Salma was expecting Guillaume's child.

So Monsieur Akhbr cut his daughter off. Guillaume was

caught up in his troubles and I saw him less and less frequently. When we did see each other, we spent long hours discussing possible solutions. His expression was sombre and his frown gave his eyes an unfathomable darkness. He had come up with a desperate plan that he had decided to put into action.

I had introduced him to my casino-going acquaintances because he had proved to be a dab hand at poker. With me as his chaperone, he joined diplomats seeking to chase away boredom, industrialists whose wildly successful business affairs deprived them of new thrills, and the local mafia godfathers, up at La Réserve, on the Corniche.

The restaurant was built on pilings and looked straight out over the ocean. Guillaume had begun going more often. Whenever he was on shore leave, he spent his days and nights playing poker. To begin with he was the casino heart-throb, everyone's favourite louche Frenchman. He had some impressive wins and he was persistent, single-minded. More than anything, he amused the regulars. And then he began to have some big wins, really big, and various people began to lose their sense of humour, notably Jean Fanchon. Fanchon, a taciturn man who was always puffing on a cigar, had an apparently murky history that had led to him leaving France in something of a hurry. He had not set foot there since 1935. Passionate about architecture by day, he was a hardnosed, unscrupulous, crooked property dealer by night. He knew everything about the Casablanca smart set, including a great deal about their private affairs. This was how he had succeeded in climbing to the upper echelons of society and creating a handsome nest egg thanks to the several mansions he owned that brought in a tidy sum. He was generally very discreet, but he always punctuated his victories with a broad smile and an exclamation: "Well, well, well! My buildings are certainly bearing fruit."

That evening, however, a glimmer of anger could be seen, reflected in Guillaume's eyes. Guillaume had borrowed some money from me, a huge sum relative to what he earned. He promised he would pay it all back. Unknown to him, I had followed him to the casino. In the gaming room, the atmosphere had changed. Guillaume's arrogant confidence electrified the air; even the sea was crashing against the props of the building with an unusual intensity. The game went on for hours as the storm grew wilder; none of the players seemed to be paying it the slightest attention. My heart was thundering in my chest. The catastrophe playing out in front of my eyes filled me with horror.

The least adventurous players, like Étienne Delalande, director of a thriving Moroccan maritime transport company affiliated to Shell, and Michel Charon, director of the head-quarters of the Moroccan Petrol Company, got up from the table like courteous losers. Lyautey's cousin played several hundred more francs, more out of curiosity than stubbornness, then towards three in the morning he too withdrew from the game.

Fanchon and Guillaume were now engaged in a fight to the death. Guillaume – I had an unimpeded view of his cards – kept changing his strategy. As soon as his adversary had worked it out, he altered it radically, catching him unawares with another winning hand. Minutes, hours went by, until sunlight pierced the heavy curtain of shadowy cloud that had veiled the darkest night of my life. The storm began to die down around dawn, as the wind dropped. Everything fell silent. Outside it was still; the sea was completely flat. Fanchon's eyes flashed. The misty glow of the sky merged with the grey-green sea. Suddenly the sound of Guillaume's voice made everybody start.

"I'll bet you your mansion on Alger Street . . ."

Loubna, 2005

I went home, alone and feeling strangely empty. As if everyone had a head start on me, and I was just a puppet. I was still awake in the living room at three in the morning, exhausted, having been ditched by my best friend and messed around by the man who was probably my only chance of seeing my dream come true. And yet all I cared about was one thing: trying to understand the logic behind the replies to Guillaume's letters.

The letters from C had been combed through by the censor with the utmost attention to detail. The more I read them, the more the phrases that had been underlined seemed familiar. Not only did they not ring true, but I felt quite certain I'd heard them before.

My mind was whirling. For crying out loud, where could I have read those words? They spoke to me; they evoked a familiar world. But like a word that sits on the tip of your tongue, they just wouldn't come into my mind.

Please, Guillaume, pull yourself together! The other night in the bar, you were so two-faced it was almost as though you were telling the truth. All your shipmates were staring at us. I'll say it again. You have to do it!

I sat in my apartment, my thoughts going round and round in circles, beside myself at my inability to figure out the key to the truth. I was positive that if I managed to work out where these words came from, I would discover who my grandfather really was. And I would finally manage to figure out the link between the wife of a British industrialist and a sleazy game of poker.

My phone rang, and I dragged myself from my thoughts. Real life was calling.

Suddenly I felt dizzy and had to sit down. I was beginning to loathe these letters, filled with sentences whose real meaning I couldn't grasp.

There was one in particular I kept going back to: *It was almost as though you were telling the truth.*

Nothing good was hidden in those words; at best they meant "traitor", at worst "Nazi spy". But it was clearly some kind of code known only to my grandfather and this woman.

Clotilde, 1940

After my husband's jealous outburst, I took to wearing a djellaba to avoid being recognized whenever I met up with Guillaume, especially when I went down to the port. But while I could no longer be identified, my presence there risked provoking increased curiosity.

One evening, as we were watching *Pépé le Moko* at the Vox, an idea sprouted in my mind. The film tells the story of a deserter, a sailor nicknamed "Moko", who comes from Toulon and is hiding from the police in the casbah in Algiers. One day he meets and falls in love with a socialite, a Parisienne, and determines to break out of his prison. All through the film I kept glancing over at Guillaume – he was too handsome, too impressive, to end up like that, to risk losing his life so young . . . he simply had to desert from the navy. When the film was over, we got into my black Citroën and I sped off in the direction of the lighthouse.

Down below, the black mass of the starlit sky was reflected in the stormy surface of the ocean. A breeze was blowing. As I drove, all I could think about was putting the finishing touches to a plan that I couldn't imagine him rejecting. The ocean opened up before us like a great possibility. Now I could see that our love had a future.

"Guillaume. You must hear me out. I've been thinking a great deal recently, and I know exactly what we have to do. You're going to jump ship. I'll get hold of new papers for you, and you'll come and work for me. My husband won't realize until it's too late. We're leaving for New York in a few days, and you will be my companion. I'll pay you well. You must leave this madness to the others. I'll drive to the port tomorrow evening, and I'll be there every day at the same time for the next week. When the moment is right, you can pretend to have an errand to run in the port. I'll pick you up. I know that deserting has serious consequences, but I beg you not to stand by your principles. Life is too short to worry about these things – even more so when you're in the navy. It's not as if they'll pay you back for your sacrifice. Look at your father: he's never got over what he went through. Is that the future you want? I know you've always wanted to travel the world, that's why I came after you, why I put pressure on my husband to be transferred to Casablanca. Don't worry, he hasn't been asking questions, and he won't. Guillaume, I will be here all next week, by your ship, waiting for you to come whistling down the gangplank, your hands in your pockets and a smile on your lips. You won't need to say a word. If we wait it will be too late. I beg you. I love you, and as you know, I prefer my lovers alive."

He smiled. Not at the sentiment, but at that last sentence. It was a reference to *Pépé le Moko*. We had devised a simple code for the letters we wrote to each other. Lines from films we'd seen together. The Jean Gabin films we were both so fond of.

He took me in his arms and we made love beneath the soft light of the stars. I took this to be his consent to my plan. But it turned out to be the last time we ever made love. It was a moment of pure joy for me, the last one, and I believed he was going to do it, even though afterwards he said, "*Adieu.* Goodbye."

After that, we sent each other a series of letters which in essence contained a single veiled question from me: *Are you coming away with me? I beg you, come with me!*

The code was simple. Most of the lines we used to communicate were from *Pépé le Moko*, *Port of Shadows*, *Daybreak* and *Coral Reefs*. In each of these films the main character is on the run, trying to escape with his lover. We knew them all by heart and therefore we knew exactly which scenes the other was referring to. "Big decisions should be taken over small carafes," I wrote, fixing a time to meet in one of those overcrowded cafés popular with sailors looking for cheap thrills to block out the world for a while. He knew what I wanted to talk about; we had no need even to bring up the subject. I remember growing frustrated with him one evening when I realized I had lost. He was determined not to give in to my plan.

The previous weeks, as the situation had been growing increasingly tense, we had begun to limit our allusions to just two films: *Pépé le Moko* and *Daybreak*. In the first film, the hero tries to escape: "You're afraid for your life?" "What do you think? It's the only one I have," we hear as Pépé decides to escape the casbah. In the second, the hero remains, waiting for daybreak, resigned, unable to flee and powerless to alter his destiny. An allusion to the first film meant that Guillaume would follow me; a mention of the second that he was going to stay. I waited impatiently for an answer to every letter. For example, he'd quote this line from *Pépé le Moko* – "You're wrong to be thinking about things. You're not used to it. That's what's giving you a headache" – when he'd decided to try and escape. But if he quoted from *Daybreak* – "When I'm with you, I can breathe a little" or "It's a wonderful thing to be loved" or "When you're ready, all you have to do is let me know" – it was a categorical refusal. It meant he had decided to stay on the ship, to remain in the navy, to sacrifice himself for Salma, to let me leave without him.

"I want to be with just one woman, Clotilde. I love her and she loves me. It's written in the stars," he told me on our last night together, in the car on the Corniche looking out over the ocean. I dreamed of his love, but in his final embrace he told me he belonged to another woman now.

And it did indeed seem to be written in the stars: Salma had fallen in love with him, too. He always wrote back to me, but it was quite clear that there was no question of him running away without her. Everything seemed to be taking a turn for the worse, both for me and Guillaume. The wind had changed, war had been declared, and he appeared to have made some long-term enemies: Fanchon, the biggest loser in the poker game; Akhbr, Salma's father; and Basri, the actual owner of the building and an associate of Fanchon and Akhbr, who sometimes handed his properties over to Fanchon to run, in the hope of making a fast buck.

Loubna, 2005

I keep thinking about the last thing that Anis said to me before he slammed the door: that I seemed to think my life was a film.

Please, Guillaume, pull yourself together! The other night in the bar, you were so two-faced it was almost as though you were telling the truth. All your shipmates were staring at us. I'll say it again. You have to do it!

Everything suddenly became clear. At last I realized what these lines made me think of: the dialogue in black and white films. Disreputable men, sailors, petty crooks, deserters . . . All those 1930s movies starring Jean Gabin began to rush through my mind.

I went and looked through all my old films. I watched the entire filmography of Jean Gabin up to 1940: *The Grand Illusion, La Bandera, Pépé le Moko, Daybreak, Port of Shadows* and *Coral Reefs*. I barely noticed the night passing and the sun beginning to rise.

For the third time in a week, I didn't sleep all night. But it was worth it, because this time my sleepless night had spawned a series of victories. Now I had a list of all the scenes alluded to in the letters. "You were so two-faced it was almost as though you were telling the truth" came from *Pépé le Moko*. "A swimmer, as far as I'm concerned, is already a drowned man": *Port of Shadows*. "A border is a thing that cannot see itself": *The Grand Illusion*. "When I'm with you, I can breathe a little": *Daybreak*.

All the mysterious phrases in the letters from C were lines from 1930s films starring Jean Gabin. All made before the death of my grandfather. This woman, C, mentioned a possible future career in cinema for him once the war was over; his actor's charisma. So it must have been a code. The lovers had both seen the same films and used the dialogue to say things that they couldn't express openly without arousing suspicion.

Once I'd worked this out it was like I'd managed to access the private world the couple had created. The nature of the code intrigued me, though. Why these films in particular, all featuring the same actor? I put all the letters C had written to Guillaume in chronological order. C must have kept the letters he had sent her in return. The last ones betrayed a sense of urgency; they were briefer and their contents darker. And, interestingly, now they only alluded to *Pépé le Moko* or *Daybreak*. I don't how my grandfather had answered these urgent questions, but she was clearly expecting him to act like a character played by Gabin: begging him to desert and run away with her, but fearing that he would stay behind and wait.

The most monumental discovery for me was that now I could be absolutely certain he hadn't been a spy, much less a traitor. He'd been preoccupied by something else. It hadn't been his own happiness he'd been thinking about, but that of this yet-to-be born child, and the woman who was carrying him – who was not the woman who had written these letters. C had referred to a rival in the letters she wrote in the final few weeks.

The building he had won in the poker game wasn't a story of ego, love of gambling, or because he'd been fraternizing with the local underworld, but to provide for my grandmother and their child. I sensed a grand gesture dictated by despair as he realized the noose was tightening around his neck. His incredible luck had cost him dear.

He wanted to escape with my grandmother, to go somewhere far away from the raging conflict. I imagine his hopes were foiled by the damn explosion.

Cracking this code confirmed what I thought I now knew

about my grandfather: he had always been crazy about the cinema. Like I was – but how was it possible, since I'd never had any way of knowing this about him, that we shared the same obsession?

My eyes filled with tears. If I hadn't been so fanatical about film history, I would never have deciphered their secret code. And at the very moment when I'd been thinking that he'd been a spy and a traitor, a collector of women – one of whom was my grandmother, whom I'd thought must have been just one more notch on his bedpost – I'd found out not only that we were both driven by the same passion, but that he had risked everything to bet on an entire building for my grandmother, the woman who was pregnant with my father.

I looked at my watch. It was five in the morning, and the last stars were fading in the sky. I decided to go for a walk in the city that belonged to me as much as it did to my beloved ghosts. I walked along Hassan II Boulevard, which used to be called Boulevard de la Gare, up to the former Square of France. I passed the Rialto, the Empire and the Café de l'Empire, and the building that had been constructed where the Vox used to be. I only had to close my eyes and I could picture it all as it would have been in my grandfather's time. Casablanca still bears traces of the 1920s alongside scars from the war. As I walked along the port, I thought about how this was where it all happened; it was another era, a time of war and violence. Here the sea is hidden behind walls, as if it were better not to know it was there. But then it reappears, there it is after all, in the air and the sunlight.

I wanted to continue tracing my grandfather's footsteps, so I carried on towards the square where Bousbir used to be, then turned towards the Ben M'sik cemetery where I found a modest grave that almost certainly didn't contain a body. It was identical to all the others, completely plain, clean and white. It had kept its secrets for decades. Until today. My past had long been shrouded in tragic shadows, and now the truth was being revealed. A shaft of sunlight broke through the cloud, seeming to sweep away the mystery once and for all. Like a homage to the moment my father was born and the moment of my grandparents' first assignation, it was once again in the early-morning light that the mystery was, at last, about to be unravelled.

Felix, 1940

We're preparing to weigh anchor in the dead of night and head out into the Atlantic. As soon as the sun comes up, we'll leave Casablanca. Things are kicking off somewhere, but I managed to post a letter to Lili earlier today. I told her what I'd discovered about her brother – that he was nowhere to be found in Casablanca, or at any rate he was not on any list drawn up by the navy or the hospitals. And that he definitely wasn't with Ginette in France, given that he'd been sighted in the port of Casablanca on the day of the explosion. I'm so sorry for Ginette. Not that she'll be the only one who'll take this hard – it won't be easy to hear for the other woman in his heart, either, the one who was so much more serious than the others. I took the opportunity of telling Lili again that she is always in my thoughts, and that getting through my tasks on board ship is like torture.

I couldn't send her the letter Clotilde gave me because the censors are bound to look through everything and I'd be asked what I'm doing with it in my possession. I don't want to get mixed up in all that.

In the end I didn't stay long in Casablanca after I'd seen Clotilde. I'd been told I was being sent to Toulon as a matter of urgency, to board *Le Fougueux*. From there we headed straight to Cherbourg, where things were heating up. That's where I was on 22 June when I heard the armistice had been signed. A little over a week later and we're still having a hard time believing it. There's panic in the ranks . . . I only got back to Casablanca yesterday, and already we're about to take off again. I hope the sea'll die down because Jesus Christ, the weather was filthy these past few days. Yet again, I thought we were done for this time. The waves were as high as the deck.

I shouldn't be spending so much time thinking about this whole sorry story, but the truth is, I can't get it out of my head. I keep thinking of something Clotilde said: "Guillaume still belongs to me in a way, because he's still in my heart." I think that's amazing, to be able to love someone so much that you don't even expect anything of them any more. You just want them to carry on breathing. Whenever I look out towards the horizon, just like he used to, Guillaume the Great, I think I almost understand what he was trying to see all the way over there.

I still haven't plucked up the courage to read his last letter, partly because I don't feel I'm worthy of reading it, and partly out of respect. It was his private life. I've held out for two weeks. But the sea, day breaking over the horizon, it makes me melancholy . . . and curious, too. You know what though, bugger it, I'll only have to pretend not to have read it. I'll keep it to myself. After giving it to Lili, I'll act all noble, promise her I didn't open it, say that it's none of my business . . . And she'll think I'm completely worthy of her and her brother. She'll be bowled over by how honourable I am, that's for sure.

I can't help but smile at my own cunning. Oh, the tricks I picked up from old Guillaume, just by watching the way he lived his life. Okay, it hasn't earned me any rewards in the navy, but I've picked up a few in real life.

What I think is that he wanted to desert, but not without Salma, and it wasn't the right moment. He never said a thing, didn't trust a soul, but you could tell something was bothering him. A military man in the middle of the war doesn't have a lot else on his mind except worrying about dying and how to avoid it. The thing is, I know it's not just friends he made among the Casablanca smart set. It's never a good idea to have enemies on both sides. That only multiplies the ways you might lose your life.

I never really believed this story about him being a spy and a traitor, partly because he was too distinguished, too honourable. But also, more importantly, I can't see him wanting to cast a shadow over the whole of the rest of his life. Because afterwards it's all very well, but you've got the rest of your days to live with all the mess from back then weighing on your conscience. You have to be able to look at yourself in the mirror. You have to be able to leave the house without being recognized. It's either the firing squad or constant vigilance. And Guillaume's dream – his real dream, the big one – had been to try his luck on the big screen . . . I don't think he'd have wanted to ruin his chances and have to spend the rest of his life in the shadows, avoiding the eyes of the generals.

I don't exactly know the end of the story, but as far as I can tell, he didn't get out and he didn't survive. He let me go on shore leave in his place that night – I don't know why, maybe he explains it in the letter – but he didn't want to run away with Clotilde. Her life was less important to him than Salma's, and I think I finally understand that.

Now I just have to wait patiently for the war to be over to find Lili and build a life with her. The next time I see her, I'll have enough things to tell her parents for them to be able to keep their imagination under control. Because when you're grieving, what's even worse than the pain is the way the mind sniffs around in the furthest corners of your memory, stumbling on fragments of images and incidents that bring you to tears, as if death alone wasn't enough.

I've experienced it with my mates who snuffed it on *La Railleuse*, at least the ones whose bodies we were able to count. For Léon, I try not to think about the return game of poker I promised him so he could try and recoup the losses he'd made the night before the explosion: "I'm on a losing streak tonight. Good job we're not on a mission – I wouldn't rate my chances!" For Gabriel, I avoid walking past the Café du Hammam, where he used to "drink a toast to death. Let the bugger put on his cloak and pick up his scythe. He doesn't scare me."

Thinking about Guillaume, however, is pretty hard to avoid. I see him everywhere, leaning over the bridge, or swaggering up to me with a wink and a fag hanging out of his mouth: "Don't think I'm going to end up a stiff, Felix! You know why? Because they call me the Comeback Kid!"

They were all so brave and so proud, but death sneaked up behind them and whispered, "Don't bet on it."

Casablanca's a desert for me now, a cemetery, empty in spite of the endless hustle and bustle . . . Now it's just a huge chasm into which my friends have fallen, one after the other. I know I'm standing on the edge of it, and it wouldn't take much for me to disappear down there too. But I've got one thing going for me: I'm a lucky bastard! You couldn't make it up, the way I've cheated death like I have. I'd like to be able to say I pulled it all off myself, but . . .

So, I'm going to do my best not to step in the shit on the path ahead; to keep being in the right place at the right time.

Now I have to say my goodbyes – we're still stuck here but not for much longer. We're waiting for the order to head out into the Atlantic. The sun's coming up, it's going to be a beautiful day, and I'm so filled with bittersweet nostalgia that I can hardly breathe. I'm doing my best to keep it together, but it's not like I have any choice in the matter: I told Lili, "I promise you won't lose both the men you love. That would be too much!" This vow I've made her is like a hand outstretched over a grave. Sometimes, it makes me forget my worries. I tell myself, "Come on, Felix, one foot in front of the other, one day at a time, it's all going to be okay. Even the war will come to an end. It has to."

But you need a little bit of fear to stay alive. Fear sharpens your wits . . . And let's face it, if Guillaume died, with all the luck he had, I don't exactly rate my chances of survival – nor those of anyone else round here.

Anyway, as I wait for orders, I can't help but look at the envelope in my hand again. Guillaume's last words . . . It's a bit like trying to bring the past back up to the surface. I keep telling myself that I shouldn't read it, that it will make me sadder than I've ever been. But of course, I just can't help myself.

> *Clotilde,*
>   *You know how much you mean to me, but I have to let you go, and you shall have to do the same. Say hello to New York for me and enjoy the wonderful life I've always dreamed of. We loved each other, but now I've met someone whose life is taking me on a different path. I saw the sun rise today, just as it has every time I have known true joy.*
>   *Guillaume*

I think about Salma again, who Clotilde told me about. It looks like he decided to stick with her. Where did they meet? I have no idea. He never took me with him on his lone-wolf jaunts.

How nicely he wrote – this is Guillaume all over. Enigmatic, deep, expressing the kind of things people don't usually say . . . Still, I don't understand what it has to do with Clotilde's parting shot about the cinema. I suppose this isn't the first time I find myself out of my depth when it comes to Guillaume's fancy words.

I must have nodded off for a few minutes. It's hot enough to make you melt now. The kind of heat that dazes you, makes you wilt . . . especially when you've no idea what's waiting for you in a few hours. But it turns out I'm not going to be left in peace . . . Me and three other sailors are being summoned by the captain. "We're changing direction, no time to spare. The dreadnought *La Bretagne* needs backup, and we're setting sail within the hour. We're no longer heading for the Atlantic, we are going to Mers el-Kébir, in Algeria." There's pandemonium in the bridge; our shipmates are talking about a marine assault. That's big. We're not going to become Krauts, we're going to fight back.

We race to pack our kitbags. We'll have to be ready in half

an hour. I'm whistling to myself and find Pierrot in our cabin.
He is lying on his camp bed, watching me. He obviously can't
believe what he is seeing. "What's up with you? You're grinning
like a madman. You that happy to be off on a mission? Fed up
of lounging around, are you?"

It's true I can't help feeling a bit smug about the turn of
events. It's not complicated: my new posting reminds me of
the lucky hand life dealt me not that long ago . . . There's
nothing better than war to make a man superstitious! And
considering what happened after I took Guillaume's shore leave,
I can't help thinking my guardian angel will get me out of any
sticky situation.

I look at Pierrot. I know I should keep my trap shut – I've
got such a big mouth, I never know when to keep it closed.
But before I know it, I sling my kitbag over my shoulder and
say: "I'm a lucky bastard, my friend. Last time there was a
change of plan I came out of it pretty well."

Loubna, 2005

Anis and I had gone for a trip into the desert. We stood there holding hands, surrounded by dunes we had never walked on before.

Now I knew almost every detail of my grandfather's story. I understood who he had been, and at last I could lay to rest my little girl's dreams.

Guillaume had fallen in love with a young woman who was much wealthier than he was. She must have been cut off by her family, which led him to bet all he had on an apartment building in a poker game. The same building in which all his descendants have lived ever since.

The day I finished putting the pieces of the puzzle together, I went over to see Anis. I wanted him to listen to me and to forgive me. He had also discovered a few things, and between us we completed the picture. When I told him about the game of poker, he said:

"The fact that he lost to your grandfather doesn't make Fanchon an honest diplomat who was fleeced by some street kid. Quite the opposite in fact: all the others had joined forces against him. Fanchon was a friend of Akhbr, who had put a private detective on his daughter and Guillaume. He wouldn't have been able to so much as wiggle his little finger without getting arrested, which he must have known. Given Ali's behaviour, it's obvious that the family still holds a grudge. I'm pretty sure that as soon as he found out who you were, Ali abandoned any intention of financing your cinema. All he wanted was to avenge what in his mind was an unacceptable affront. Anyway, it's clear your grandfather had a gift for attracting bad luck.

He managed to make enemies of the three most powerful men in the Casablanca underworld at the time: Akhbr, Basri and Fanchon. It makes you wonder if the explosion wasn't planned with the express intention of finishing him off. I don't suppose we'll ever know. But the war certainly helped their interests, firstly by providing cover for their smuggling activities and all kinds of dodgy consortiums, and then because the settling of scores could be disguised as wartime incidents."

I'm going to have to live with this unresolved mystery. All those enigmatic letters, filled with lovers' promises and confessions of passion, hold secrets that will never give themselves up.

Anis held me closer to him. We had got up very early to see the spectacular sunrise over the desert. It was magnificent, majestic – utterly worth getting up in the middle of the night to watch the sun lighting up the dunes, licking the ground with a tongue of flame.

Standing facing the sea of amber sand, I felt dizzy all of a sudden. It looked like memory itself: aglow, filled with mysteries and promises for the future.

Barely had the war begun and Guillaume's family had been blown apart. They had lost almost everything. So few people remained alive.

After Guillaume died, they had to deal with his absence. They had to live with the memory of a boy who would never grow up to be a man. A promise that would never be kept. I guess the war stole a little more of their life force from them every day, and my father and I had grown up in the shadow of their broken-hearted incomprehension.

At the last minute, Guillaume had decided not to desert. He felt duty-bound to remain in Casablanca with my grandmother Salma and my not-yet-born father Tarek, "morning light", a belly swollen with the promise of a bright new life.

Before he met Salma, Guillaume had been a youthful Lothario, with lovers from all different walks of life; a slightly shady collector of charms who stole women's hearts. He'd dreamed of becoming a film star.

Anis slipped his hand in mine and gave me a smile I'd never seen before. But I had always known that light in his eyes.

As a teenager, before he enlisted in the navy, Guillaume, dreaming with all his heart of seeing the world, had been in a hurry to discover what lurked beyond the horizon, excited and impatient to see for himself what exotic splendours were out there.

Anis gently touched my cheek, on the exact spot where I could feel the first rays of sun warming my face. My skin recognized his touch. Our love had grown up in the midst of these secrets.

No longer a child, and not yet a grown man, Guillaume had made a promise to a young woman that he would return home to her. Eventually the wind blew that promise away like a mote of dust. How could he have known then that his life would be elsewhere?

Anis placed his lips on mine and I lost all sense of time as it began to slip away in reverse.

Hélène, 1940

There was nothing that amused Guillaume more when he was a child than pinching the cherries out of his sister's pie, or a glass of brandy from his father's stock down in the cellar, or the first slice of plum tart. On the other hand he would never have dreamed of touching anything of mine, which is how I know that it can't have been he who took down all his letters from the walls and ceiling in the attic. Lili, perhaps? Maybe she was jealous and wanted to show me I was ignoring her and devoting all my attention to her brother. Or could it have been Lucien, for the same reason? From now on things are going to be just how they used to be.

What a wonderful child Guillaume was. I can still picture him learning to walk and to write, and the first time I caught him gazing hungrily at the horizon. We were on holiday in Tréport. That was where he learned to swim, quite fearlessly – after only a few days, he jumped into the cold, grey sea, happy as anything. That was how he approached everything, how he made his way through life: fearlessly, head first. That was how he drove the first time, nearly getting us all killed one May Sunday. That was how he invited Ginette out dancing, when just a week earlier he'd barely been able to manage two steps. He spotted her and knew he would see her again the following week: "Mother, teach me!" It became an obsession: he had to be able to dance better than any other potential suitor. Frowning, and totally unable to follow the steps with any grace, nonetheless he kept practising. According to Étienne, Lili and their friends, he rose to the occasion rather well.

I look at him today, back from that terrible war, sitting in the kitchen in his sailor's uniform, and I ache to ask him to dance with me again, my little boy.

For days now, Lili and Lucien have been cursing Ginette, who ran off with Etienne to have his child. Lili keeps saying she hopes that "all their wishes and dreams collapse like a house of cards". It's crazy, all the fancy phrases she knows. Guillaume will get over it. She didn't deserve him anyway. I can see he's not at all upset by it. At his age, it won't take him long to meet someone else and fall in love again.

I managed to keep from shouting with joy when he turned up, so I could have him to myself for a bit longer, until the two of them stopped obsessing. I'm so ashamed of Lucien and Lili! There they are, as if they're at a wake. Staring at my little boy as if he were a stranger, as if he doesn't belong here, or as if he has turned up only to announce he's leaving again for good. The proof is, he's here. Soon, when we're alone together again, I'll be able to tell him how much I love him. I always knew he'd survive.

I have to concentrate on my dressmaking now. I'm behind, and we have the rest of our lives ahead of us to be together, now he's home – alive, actually alive! He's thinner, perhaps; his cheeks have lost their roundness, and he seems smaller somehow, but that's because he hasn't eaten properly for so long, and because he was so afraid. His eyes are lighter but otherwise he looks just the same. He is less affectionate than he was, as well. He won't let me take him in my arms, and Lucien stops me from trying. Lili can't stop crying, looking at me as if I've ruined her wedding. But I know all this will pass. They've forgotten how to be happy, that's all.

Lili keeps wailing that Felix won't come back from Mers el-Kébir, crying that their love was just a shooting star, the kind that causes the most pain because it doesn't have time to disappoint, even a tiny bit.

I've left her alone to calm down; she keeps pushing me away when I offer a hug or comforting words. She thinks I don't understand. But I know he will return one day. The world is vast and war cages men, but it won't go on forever.

Guillaume stands there in his sailor's uniform, his face stricken at the sight of his sister's sorrow. Not so long ago he would have taken her in his arms to comfort her, but violence and fear have made him forget the simplest gesture of love. But that too will pass. Men who have been to war lose their compassion; their bodies come home first, before their hearts do. Guillaume's heart remains in Casablanca, but it will be back soon, I know. They call him the Comeback Kid.